God's Playbook

God has a game plan for our lives.
It is up to us to execute the plays
in God's playbook.

Other Books by Sunnie Day

When Delilah Smiles

Sunnie and Her Peeps

The Insignificant Penny

Train to Nowhere

Au revoir Stilettos

The Magical Victrola

The Reluctant Good Son

Sunnie's Inanimates Speak

Coming Soon

Saving Bluebell

God's
PLAYBOOK

Walking By Faith

... A Novel

Laurus **BOOKS**

God's PLAYBOOK

By Kevin Kruise and
Kimberly Kruise Thompson (aka Sunnie Day)

Paperback: ISBN-13: 978-1-938526-24-4
E-Book: ISBN-13: 978-1-938526-25-1

Edited by Cynthia Marts | The Laurus Company

Cover by Jennifer Tipton Cappoen | The Laurus Company

Published by LAURUS BOOKS

Printed in the United States of America

LAURUS BOOKS
P. O. Box 894
Locust Grove, GA 30248 USA
www.TheLaurusCompany.com

Laurus Books is an imprint of The Laurus Company. This book may be purchased in paperback from TheLaurusCompany.com, Amazon.com, BarnesandNoble.com, and other retailers around the world. Also available in eBook format for the Kindle, iPad, and Nook.

Dedication

This book is dedicated to our parents,

Hershel and Dahlas Kruise

Without them, this book may never have come to pass. We are blessed to have two loving parents who have stood behind us—mistakes and all—as we grew up from children to adults. Their consistent encouragement, love, and support have truly been God's Playbook in our lives. We love you, Mom and Dad.

—Kim and Kevin

Our Friend

Always present in the time of need.
Always listening, but never silent.
Tells you what is necessary,
not only what you want to hear.
Never rejects you, does not judge you,
and never leaves you.
When you feel alone, he is watching, waiting.
The Holy Spirit is there.
He is our friend.

— Kevin Kruise, 2012

Table of Contents

Table of Contents

Foreword

Decisions are made in life every day, but few realize at that moment in time how that decision could alter their destiny. Some people may call it fate; but Christian believers call it faith. Certainly one can believe that life and its circumstances just happen—*que sera sera*—whatever will be, will be. However, faith is much bigger than that. It challenges our perceptions, our free will, our hope, and our endurance to overcome obstacles. Walking by faith is not a process for the faint of heart, nor is it temporal or selective. It is an enduring lifestyle.

God's playbook for our lives was designed from the beginning of time. It does not guarantee a life without hurts and problems, nor does it guarantee perfect bliss. It does promise us a never-ending love from God. It gives us hope when there seems to be no hope. Our lives become a tapestry made of many colors, sewn together, intertwining lives in ways we could never imagine.

Thomas Mitchell and Sandy Goodman were high

school sweethearts since the 9th grade. Like most kids their age, they had hopes, dreams, and career ambitions. Never did they imagine that their relationship and faith would be shaken to the point that their hopes and dreams could be shattered. Thomas and Sandy are faced with circumstances beyond their control, and their faith in God is put to the test.

Thomas and Sandy must overcome their circumstances and soon realize that God places people in their path who enable them to find the true meaning of faith. God has a game plan for our lives, and it is up to us to execute the plays in God's playbook.

Chapter One

✳

The Playbook

*O*nly two hours from St. Louis, Missouri, nestled in the Ozark Highlands along historic Route 66 lays the quaint little town of St. James. St. James is no different than most small towns; its citizens are proud of their community, everyone is known by their first name, a stranger stands out in the crowd, and Friday night football games are the talk of the town. But it is the faith in God and the love of family and community that receive the highest acclaim from visitors passing through.

Thomas Mitchell and Sandy Fogel had lived in St. James all their young lives, and had never had to travel far to find adventure. The occasional weekend trip to St. Louis to shop in the big city, catching a St. Louis Cardinals baseball game, boating at the Lake of the Ozarks, or even just a summer picnic at Maramec Spring Park, were all pleasant family outings they grew up loving. Most of these trips were even taken together. In fact, except for the occasional family vacation, Thomas and Sandy were rarely seen apart while they were growing up.

Anyone that knew them well enough valued the simple love and adoration they shared for one another. It seemed that they were seamlessly connected in soul and spirit. And although their future professional interests were different, they were certain that they were stronger together than apart. So after their high school graduation, they both decided to attend St. Louis University, so they could stay close to home, and each other, while still following their own paths.

Thomas's parents, Thomas Sr. and Luetta Mitchell, owned and operated a winery in St. James. "La Vite," which translated to "The Vine," was a winery that was not just a family business, but a sanctuary of long-standing traditions passed down from many Italian descendants who settled in St. James in the early 1800s.

Sandy's parents were both part of the city's legal system. Her father, Edward, was the city's district attorney, and her mother, Elizabeth, was an attorney who specialized in real estate law with a firm in St. James.

Naturally, the elder Mitchells and Fogels were hoping their children would follow the same paths as they had, but they understood that the road they took may not lead to the same destination as theirs. After all, they understood that God creates and manages life's playbook, and sometimes He allows us to call the plays, whether they are right or wrong.

And though their lives weren't always easy, their strife often led them down the right path. Sandy's first brush with heartache came when she was only seven. That year, her younger brother, Stephen, died of Leukemia. It was a time that brought many changes, but somehow the family was able to draw strength from God's love. When she saw her little brother's amazing display of courage against all odds, young Sandy was deeply inspired. She told her parents that she wanted to become a doctor, and help children that had cancer, like Stephen.

Thomas's parents had always encouraged Thomas to become a doctor as well, but Thomas had other ambitions, particularly in the field of engineering. Throughout his youth, he stood by his passions and, while they still had hopes of Thomas becoming a doctor, his parents stepped aside, allowing him to make his own decisions.

So in the fall of 2007, Thomas and Sandy entered their first semester at St. Louis University. As typical first year students, they were filled with excitement and fear. Thomas was an aspiring Aeronautical Engineer, and Sandy pursued a degree in Biology, with the hope of later being accepted into medical school.

With their classes and schoolwork leaving very little space in their schedules, they didn't always have as much time together as they'd like, and their new environments often made them uncomfortable. Dormitory life was loud, over-crowded, and full of unusual, un-Christian behaviors, the likes of which Thomas and Sandy were not used to being exposed. Whenever they had the opportunity, they would escape to the campus pizza and sub shop and talk about the good, bad, and ugly of it all. Suffice it to say that there were plenty of these occasions.

In spite of the challenges, they managed to make it through one semester after the next. Almost as quickly as it began, graduation from SLU arrived, and they faced a new phase of life: adulthood. Wide-eyed and full of anticipation, they discussed what would come next, and they discussed getting married.

"We are in love," they thought. "Our careers are about to blossom, and there is no reason to wait! Our parents married young, and they did pretty well. Why shouldn't we do the same? Of course, they'll approve of our engagement."

They decided to tell their parents about their decision on Graduation Day. Although Thomas hadn't asked Sandy for her hand formally, it was something they had talked about again and again. They were certain that it was the right thing to do.

On Graduation Day, Thomas and Sandy met their parents at the Visitor's Center and walked a few blocks up the street to the auditorium. The moment was upon them to break the news, and they couldn't contain their excitement.

Thomas spoke up first, "Mom, Dad, Mr. and Mrs. Fogel, Sandy and I have decided to get married!"

If there was ever a moment when time stood still, this was it. The group was speechless, and they didn't look happy. It was not the response the young couple had anticipated. Totally caught off-guard, their parents did their best to maintain their composure, but agreed it would be best to talk about it after the graduation ceremony. Even if everything appeared right about their relationship at the moment, they were still young and had only begun to realize the difficulties that lay ahead.

Do you remember Gods playbook? In sports, that's called an "audible." The families weren't too fond of what they were seeing, and suggested a new play.

Chapter Two

�֎

The Job Offer

*T*homas and Sandy heeded their parents' advice and agreed to wait awhile before they got married, at least until they achieved their educational goals and were secure in their jobs. Thomas had graduated with honors at SLU and was quickly hired into an Aeronautical Engineer Apprentice position with the Bastrop Corporation in St. Louis. Thomas knew that Bastrop had been a reputable company within the defense industry for over 30 years, and provided the best option for eventually getting a permanent position with a higher salary.

After passing all her medical exams, Sandy was accepted into the SLU School of Medicine in pursuit of a Doctorate in Medicine. She was on her way to becoming a Pediatric Oncologist. Inspired by her determination,

Thomas decided that as long as Sandy was going to school, he would do the same. Thinking about what was best for his career, he decided to pursue a dual-graduate degree in Aviation and Aeronautical Engineering. He found that he could do most of his classes online, which gave him a lot of time to focus on work. He hoped that this would give him a unique qualification for an executive position in the future.

In spite of the temptation to share a home, and the frequent ribbing by friends and co-workers, Thomas and Sandy agreed to live in separate apartments until they were married. Their parents had always been traditionalists, and they knew they would never support the idea of living together before their wedding.

Thomas soon found a small, one-bedroom apartment in Kirkwood, an up and coming suburb of St. Louis that was only a short commute to his new job. Sandy lived in an efficiency apartment within walking distance of the school, as well as the medical center where she studied and would later conduct clinical rotations.

In spite of their horrendous school and work schedules, they remained hopeful, knowing that a comfortable level of financial security was clearly in sight. Most of all, they were young professionals doing what they loved, which made the challenges all the more worthwhile. It would only be a couple more years until their goals would be realized and they could get married. Then they could live a long, happy, and prosperous life together. Everything was going well, and their plan was picture perfect.

The next few years were uneventful. Thomas had finished his Graduate program and had been given a part-time position at Bastrop. He was now extremely hopeful about a possible promotion to full time. Sandy was finishing up her Doctorate and had just begun her first year of Residency at the hospital.

About nine-thirty one morning, Thomas received a telephone call from the Bastrop Division Secretary telling him that he had a required appointment to see Mr. Ted Danforth promptly at 3:30 that afternoon. Mr. Danforth was the Chief Executive Officer of Bastrop Corporation and was very reputable in the Engineering, Design, and Modeling industry.

Thomas had heard that Mr. Danforth was an honorable man but was tough as nails. Although Thomas had always carried a confidence within that had been instilled by his parents, notification of this meeting immediately stirred self-doubt. He was incredibly anxious at the news and immediately broke out in a cold sweat. He reasoned to himself that he had proven to his supervisors and co-workers that he was deserving of a higher position. This could be the promotion he'd been waiting for.

Being a prompt employee, Thomas made sure he arrived at Mr. Danforth's office early. At exactly 3:25, the secretary notified Mr. Danforth that Thomas had arrived for his appointment. Within moments, she motioned him toward the office door with a smile.

Nearing the thick, wooden door, he straightened his tie, took a few deep breaths, wiped the sweat from his brow, and knocked.

"Come in," Mr. Teddy Danforth replied in a strong, rather deep tone.

Slowly, Thomas entered the spacious office. The smell of fresh coffee lingered throughout the room. Huge windows formed a 90-degree angle from one corner of the office to the other, providing a brilliant semi-panoramic view of downtown St. Louis. In the distance, Thomas could see the famous St. Louis Gateway Arch and the mighty Mississippi River flowing at its base. He gazed around the room again, taking in everything—the comfortable sofa near the door, surrounded by ornate bookshelves, the small, thick wooden table against the far wall, the photographs and models of concept aircrafts hung on the walls. The room had a warm, comfortable feeling that made Thomas think of log cabins and blazing hearths.

I could have an office like this one day, he thought to himself.

"Have a seat, Mr. Mitchell," Mr. Danforth said in his booming voice. He was an imposing man, with thick, dark hair and a stern face.

Thomas sat down in a plush, black leather chair facing Mr. Danforth. Folding his hands on his lap and then quickly unclasping them, he attempted to get comfortable in the large, overstuffed chair. He quickly realized that he was fidgeting and thought to himself, *Calm down, Thomas. Don't blow it!* But Mr. Danforth hadn't even looked up yet. After shuffling through a stack of papers on his desk, he raised his head and studied Thomas carefully for what seemed like forever to Thomas.

After what seemed like several minutes, Mr. Danforth finally spoke. "The reason I have called you here is to congratulate you on successfully working so long with our company and becoming such a valuable employee. Only a select few make it this far after so little time. You have shown that you are more than capable of doing the job, and doing it well."

He paused for a moment, and Thomas took the opportunity to speak up, "Thank you, sir. I really appreciate that."

Mr. Danforth nodded and continued, "With that said, I would like to offer you a new, full-time position on our Engineering staff. It will require more time, more responsibilities, and of course, will include a higher salary. How do you feel about that?"

Thomas could barely contain his excitement. This was what he had been waiting for. He took a deep breath, knowing he had to remain cool and collected. Thomas was rarely ever speechless, but this time he struggled to get the words to come out.

"Ye-e-ss," he said, his voice cracking. He cleared his throat and tried again, "Yes, Sir, I am honored to accept the position!"

Mr. Danforth stood, extending his hand to congratulate Thomas. Thomas followed suit, standing and raising his hand. But the next few words seemed like they came out in slow motion as their hands came close, "Please see my secretary, and she will give you travel instructions for relocating to Beijing, China."

Thomas froze, his hand hovering only inches from Mr. Danforth's. He wasn't quite certain he had heard him clearly. He hoped he *hadn't* heard him clearly.

"Excuse me, sir?" His voice sounded weak.

Certainly, there are things in life that are worth repeating, but Thomas wasn't sure he even wanted to hear this news again.

"Sir? I mean, may I ask you what you mean, sir?"

Mr. Danforth looked very serious. His brows furrowed, and Thomas could tell he was not accustomed to repeating himself.

"Mr. Mitchell," he started again, "please see my secretary. She will give you travel instructions for relocating to Beijing, China."

Thomas had heard correctly the first time, but he still didn't want to admit it. His heart began to beat faster, putting Thomas into panic mode. Thomas could hardly believe what this would mean. He was beside himself, his thoughts racing, his body beginning to tremble. He closed his eyes for a moment, taking the time to collect his thoughts.

Mustering some courage, he stated, "Mr. Danforth, I was under the impression that I could work here in St. Louis. I was not anticipating having to relocate."

Mr. Danforth watched him carefully, "Is there a problem, Thomas?"

Thomas shook his head quickly and leaned forward, closing the space between them, and shook hands with

Mr. Danforth across his desk. In an uncertain tone, he said, "No, sir. Thank you for the consideration. This would be a great opportunity. Thank you."

What else could I have said, he thought to himself as he turned away. The whole thing was quite a shock, and he had no idea how to take it in, not to mention breaking the news to Sandy. In a daze, Thomas walked slowly past the secretary without stopping or saying a word. He felt completely blindsided by the news and needed to talk to Sandy before making any decisions at all.

It was getting late that afternoon, and Sandy was still working. Her hair was pulled back and her eyes were getting tired, but still she looked diligently over the medical records of the children admitted to the Bob Costas Cancer Center at the Cardinal Glennon Children's Medical Center. She had been going over them all afternoon. She was searching for insights into the patient's medical conditions, which, hopefully, would make it easier to meet and talk with them. Sandy had always felt that it was a calling from God to work with kids. It was not long ago that God had called her to this profession through her own life's trials and tribulations, as it is with so many others who are brought to their life's work.

But tonight Sandy couldn't focus. Her mind continued drifting off to those sad, final days with Stephen. He had been such a precious little boy. He had curly blond hair, big blue eyes, and a smile that always melted her heart.

She still remembered watching her mother's heart shatter into a million pieces and the helplessness she had felt. She remembered all those days sitting by her little brother's side, playing games with him in his hospital bed, or comforting her parents the best she could.

At the time, Sandy had no idea how to deal with her own pain. But as they pulled through it, she had promised her mother that one day she would work to help other children. She could still remember the night Stephen went to be with the Lord. Her mother had just stepped out for a moment when Stephen had looked up at her with those beautiful blue eyes.

"Sissy, don't be sad. I'm not scared," he said, his voice weak but so full of love.

For the rest of her life, Sandy would see that look on Stephen's face as he closed his eyes, stepping into eternity with Jesus.

Sandy's phone suddenly rang, pulling her out of her thoughts and back into the present. "Hi, Mom, how are you?" she said after glancing at the Caller ID. "Is anything wrong?"

"No, darling. Everything is okay. I just wanted to check up on you since it has been a whole week since we last talked! You know how I get if I don't hear from you."

"Yeah," Sandy said, smiling a little. "Everything's fine here."

"Good! Well, Dad and I are thinking about coming over next weekend and wanted to know if that was okay."

"Mom, you know you don't even have to ask! Well,

actually, now that I think about it, that isn't exactly true. Let me speak with Thomas first and see if he has anything planned."

"Okay, sweetheart. Give me a call back, and let me know for sure."

"I will, Mom."

"I love you."

Sandy paused. Whenever she became weary from her studies, she would look at the photograph of Stephen that she kept with her as a constant reminder to keep pursuing her dream in spite of the hardships.

"Uh, Mom," she said after a moment, "I was just thinking about Stephen. He has been on my mind today."

There was another brief pause.

"Me, too, love. His birthday is coming up, and it's always a hard time of year. I miss him so much," Sandy's mom said finally.

"I was looking through some medical records today. So many children are suffering from cancer. It's so sad."

She paused again, then whispered, "Mom, I hope I can do this."

"Honey," her mother said, her voice firm with love and assurance, "I have no doubt that you are exactly where God has placed you. He will give you the tools you need and prepare your heart for the work that is before you. All you need to do is trust Him."

"Thanks, Mom. I love you!"

"I love you, too. See you soon, darling."

As Sandy hung up the phone, she felt like her spirit

was renewed. The encouraging words from her mother were just what she needed to make her feel as if she could do everything needed. She could walk this journey that God had called her to do.

Sandy looked up at the clock, realizing with a start that it was far later than she'd thought, and her shift had been over for more than an hour. She put the files away, clocked out, and headed home, stopping at the grocery store around the corner first.

Unlocking the front door, Sandy could hear the phone ringing. Thinking it was Thomas, she hurried. He always worried about her when she was running late. Placing the bag of groceries on the counter, she ran to answer the phone, "Hello?"

"Hi, honey. It's me," Thomas said. Sandy frowned automatically, sure that something about his voice was off. "We have to talk. Can I come over now?"

Sandy could hear an urgency in Thomas's voice that she wasn't used to, "Of course, I just made it in. Why don't we have dinner here at the apartment?"

"Um, sure," he said, not sounding very excited.

"Do hamburgers and fries sound good?"

"That sounds fine."

Sandy paused, "You sound worried. Do you want to give me a hint about what's going on?"

"I don't want to tell you over the phone. I will be there in about an hour. I love you."

He hung up without waiting for a response, and Sandy put down the receiver, immediately concerned. *What is bothering Thomas so much that he can't tell me over the phone? We have always been open and honest with each other, no matter what.*

Thomas arrived around six-thirty. He looked miserable, with his hair a mess and a deep frown on his face. He barely paused to say hello, only giving Sandy a quick hug and kiss. They headed into the living room and sat down. Thomas fidgeted, staring at his hands. It was difficult to look directly into Sandy's eyes. With some trouble, he started to explain what had happened that morning, and the job opportunity in Beijing. He desperately needed to know how Sandy felt about this major news.

He did his best to describe the meeting with Mr. Danforth and everything that had been said. Sandy sat patiently, listening to every word but feeling a bit overwhelmed. This wasn't the kind of news she had expected to hear. She did her best to see the good in all of it, but she still couldn't bring herself to accept it. There were so many questions she wanted to ask, and she was filled with fear and worry.

There were so many questions that she was afraid to ask, and she wasn't even sure Thomas could answer them. How would their relationship hold up if they were separated by thousands of miles? Would she be able to pursue her career if she went with him? Why couldn't he find a job somewhere else? How would their parents feel about it?

After he had finished and the shock had settled, Thomas and Sandy agreed to pray about it and see how God would lead them. Still unsettled but at a temporary decision, they went on with their evening.

After a quiet dinner, Thomas left to go back to his apartment. When she was finally alone, Sandy curled up on the couch, dimmed the lights, and pondered everything in her heart.

She closed her eyes and silently offered a prayer to the Lord, "God, you know our hearts. You understand how it feels to be separated from someone you love. Nevertheless, we want to see your will be done in our lives, not our own. Please help us through this."

When Thomas arrived at his apartment, he tossed his keys on the counter, took off his jacket, and loosened his tie. Leaning against the wall, he took a deep breath, offering a prayer of his own, "Lord, I need you now. I have always needed you in my life, but never like I do now. You hold my life in your hands. Give me wisdom to know what to do. Let your will be done."

If Thomas and Sandy had learned anything in their lives, it was to seek God first, trusting Him in all things. They both struggled with the idea of being separated from each other, perhaps for months or possibly even years. They had plans for their lives, even though they weren't immediate. On this night, they both wondered how long it would be before God would answer their prayers.

Chapter Three

�֎

The Patient

The next day, Sandy was again scanning through piles of medical records when a picture of a little boy caught her attention. Without knowing why, this boy captured her heart. She skimmed his file, turning all of her attention to him. His name was Micah.

Although his picture reflected a weak and fragile boy, she could tell he had a smile that would light up a room. He was only twelve years old. *Wow, this is incredible,* Sandy thought to herself. *How could a child who has been stricken with cancer at such a young age have anything to smile about?* She thought of Stephen. He had displayed such a joyful heart. Even in the very end, when he closed his eyes for the last time, he had left this earth with a smile on his face.

Here I am laboring over a non-life-threatening decision, while this little boy could be dying, Sandy thought to herself.

She suddenly felt conflicted, ashamed, and brutally selfish. The intense inspiration that she grew up with after Stephen's death washed over her anew. She could feel it all over again—the strong desire to help and to heal, all the reasons why she had wanted to become a doctor in the first place. She thought of all the wonderful physicians and nurses who surrounded her family when her little brother was sick and how she wanted to be one of those people one day, helping children in such desperate need.

As she thought about Stephen, she was reminded of the many pictures her mother used to receive each month from the St. Jude Children's Research Hospital. For as long as Sandy could remember, her mother had supported St. Jude. Even when she couldn't afford to support them financially, they were in her prayers. After Stephen died, this was her mom's way of giving to others while honoring Stephens's life.

"These kids need our prayers," she would often tell Sandy. Sandy smiled. Sometimes it was obvious exactly where Sandy got her love for children from. Her mother had taken on the cares of the world concerning these little ones and carried a burden for them by being their prayer warrior every day.

Sandy remembered the monthly check her parents would send for cancer research, supporting children who needed cancer treatments, or helping the parents who were unable to cover medical expenses. It was such a worthy cause, and she was sure it was another reason for her passion and calling to become a pediatrician.

Each time Sandy's mother received a new letter in the mail, she would say a prayer for the child before she slipped a check into the envelope, feeling the small sum of money they gave each month was the least they could do. It may have seemed insignificant to some people, but it was something very special to her parents, not to mention the children they served. Her mother would then take the picture and gently place it in her Bible as a reminder to pray for them.

Bless the LORD, O my soul, and forget not all His benefits: Who forgives all your iniquities, Who heals all your diseases, Who redeems your life from destruction, Who crowns you with lovingkindness and tender mercies, Who satisfies your mouth with good things, So that your youth is renewed like the eagle's. —Psalm 103:2-5

Thomas sat down in his office chair and turned on his computer. He had already received several emails congratulating him on his new position, and each brought a bigger lump to his throat. He looked over at his phone with a sigh, the big red eye of the voice-mail alert blinking at him, but he didn't really feel like checking it. It would probably be more congratulations about a job he didn't really want to take.

He mumbled to himself, "Why does such a good

opportunity make me feel so horrible?"

With a groan he lifted his arms over his head, stretching his neck and back.

"I need my morning pick me up. A good ol' cup of joe should fix me right up!"

The office break area was located just down the hall and was always full of employees standing in line to get their daily dose of caffeine and sugar. Thomas was a regular patron. The smorgasbord of coffee amazed Thomas. It was almost like a miniature Starbucks. He made it a point to try a different brew each day to satisfy his curiosity. He liked to think that one day he would be just a little more educated about the finer points of coffee types.

Although Thomas had been on the job for a little over a year, he still did not know everyone by name. Most of the time it was a simple "hello" or "how are you" in passing. As luck would have it, today when he was leaving the break room, he nearly collided with a co-worker brushing past him. Managing to stop just short of spilling his cup of coffee on him, Thomas was embarrassed realizing it was Mr. Edward Freeman, Director of the Human Resources Division. *Of all people, I almost dump my coffee on the one who is sending me to China,* he thought. *Then again, maybe I should make a better attempt to actually spill my coffee on him next time.*

Thomas did not know at the time that there were uncanny similarities between them. Only ten years prior, Mr. Freeman was in the same position as Thomas, with the same career ambitions. He was a young, ambitious professional and very intelligent, top of his class at New York University. He, too, used the apprenticeship program to get his foot in the door and found himself quickly ascending the corporate ladder. Now he was a Division Director at the age of 34!

It was about ten-thirty in the morning when Sandy finished reviewing all the medical records. As she put the last record back in its folder, a slim young woman at the nurses' station approached her.

"Hello, I'm here to visit my little boy in Room 305," she said. Then, with a small frown, she added, "I don't recall seeing you here before. Have you been here long?"

"No, ma'am," Sandy said, putting her hand out in greeting, "This is my second day. I'm one of the student resident doctors."

"Oh! I'm sorry for being so rude," the woman replied, taking her hand gently. "My name is Maggie. It's good to meet you! We have been so blessed to have such wonderful doctors here who have such a tremendous passion for kids. My son, Micah, is a patient here, and they have been wonderful to him."

"Did you say your son's name is Micah?" Sandy asked in surprise. "I just reviewed his medical record. He seems like a very strong boy. How long has he been here at the hospital?"

"Well, this time, he's been here for a week receiving

treatment for the RMS. But it's all been touch and go for a while now. I don't know all the medical terminology and explanations, but my Micah has been a brave little boy through it all."

Sandy watched Maggie's face, smiling thoughtfully, "Maggie, I will make it a point to go see Micah as soon as I can. It was so nice to meet you!"

"Wonderful! I'm sure he would love to meet you. He's such a trooper!"

Sandy began to think about the surprise encounter. *Was it really just a coincidence meeting Micah's mother the instant I finished looking at his medical record? Or was this a divine appointment?*

She felt compelled to learn more about Micah's cancer. It was called Rhabdomyosarcoma, with the nickname "RMS," or "rhabdo" for short. She knew that *rhabdo* meant "rod-shaped" and *myo* meant "muscle," so this cancer was considered to be a cancer of the muscles that are attached to the bones.

Sandy decided that she would study up on it tonight and go see Micah first thing in the morning.

Later that afternoon, while working on some final details on the new Airbus 9000 aircraft design, Thomas decided he could wrap things up for the day. He enjoyed working with his design team. They were all true professionals and were always willing to answer the many questions Thomas had. He was the rookie of the group when it came to hands-on work and often had more than a few queries.

As Thomas approached the doorway, he suddenly had a different idea. Without really thinking, he turned and headed over to see André Kitchens, another aircraft engineer whom he had confided in many times. The two were very similar, and Thomas trusted Andre's knowledge of the industry. They even discussed things about God quite often. Although they did not always see eye to eye on doctrine and biblical theology, they always managed to make their individual points without rubbing each other the wrong way.

"André, can I ask you a question?" Thomas asked as he approached the bench where André was working.

"Sure, bud, what's up?"

"You know I have been struggling with this whole notion of moving to China. I know it is a tremendous opportunity, but I can't seem to shake my doubts about it. What do you think I should do?"

André could sense where this was going, so he chose his words carefully. Setting his pencil down on the blue-print-covered table and removing his glasses, André said, "Thomas, one thing I do know is this: you would not be here in the first place if God had not directed your path. Continue to trust in Him. He will not lead you astray. God can open doors that no man can open. And if He can open them, He can surely close them, too!"

Thomas let out a sigh of relief. It felt good to confide in a Christian brother and get an answer that felt right.

"Thanks, my friend. See you in the morning."

As he headed off again, Thomas contemplated what André had said. He had needed to hear words of encouragement and knew in his heart that André was right.

As Thomas made his way to the elevator, he offered up a quick prayer, "Forgive me, Lord, for letting my faith be shaken, but please give me an answer soon!"

Thomas was not always as patient as he should have been, and soon he would find out that life does not always give us what we want when we want it.

Later that evening, Thomas and Sandy met for dinner at their favorite restaurant, a steakhouse in Kirkwood called Citizen Kane's. The huge array of entrée selections, side dishes, and desserts, not to mention the impeccable service, fascinated them. It was a casual, blue jean atmosphere, but it was still a lovely and elegant place to dine.

Over dinner, they discussed the events of their day. Sandy talked about Micah and meeting his mother, Maggie, while Thomas talked about the near mishap with the Director of Human Resources, Mr. Freeman, and what could have happened if it had turned into a big mess after all.

After their meal, Thomas and Sandy went back to their respective apartments for the evening. Thomas had only one more week before he had to decide whether he would accept the job in China. If not, he'd probably be looking for a job elsewhere. He knew he couldn't put off letting his boss know his intentions much longer.

Certainly, there had to be a breakthrough in their

situation eventually. *When* and *how* were the questions they were both asking. Thomas and Sandy were both learning that life can be tricky, even for a Christian believer. Do we take our hands off the situation, believing God will bring his plan into action? Do we listen to those gentle urgings that the Lord may give to move in a certain direction?

Perhaps we do both.

We trust God to move on our behalf as we walk, listening to his voice telling us to move this way or that, trusting in his leading. Thomas and Sandy were walking in this very life lesson, and would soon learn how to walk with God.

Chapter Four

✳

My Name is Micah

Thomas and Sandy had always planned to have children of their own one day, but they had agreed to wait a year or two after they were married. "Careers first," Thomas would chant to his mother after a bout of nagging.

Since Thomas and Sandy came from rather large families with loving parents, it seemed a natural progression that after their careers were established, they would have children. Their parents, being aspiring grandparents, had a tendency to keep the pressure on Thomas and Sandy to have children right away once they got married. But right now, it was the last thing the young couple was thinking about.

With all this in mind, they did not have the heart to break the news to their parents about China, and both agreed that they would let them know when the time was right. Sandy's heart stayed with the children at the hospital, while Thomas focused on finding a way to keep his job without going to China.

The next morning, Sandy was rushing around the apartment trying to get ready. Thomas would be there any minute to pick her up. She rarely ever ran late, but last night had proven to be a very restless night. Throughout the night, she had tossed and turned, waking up every few hours and seeing Micah's face. Sometimes she would get up and pace the apartment, an unsettling feeling lurking in her spirit. She was absolutely sure it was concerning this little boy.

Sandy had prayed off and on during the night, "Dear Lord, please be with Micah tonight." And she prayed as she continued to get ready. She did not know why, but there was a deep connection in her heart to this child.

Suddenly there was a knock at the door. "Morning, sunshine!" Thomas said enthusiastically when she opened the door. He was leaning against the doorframe with a big smile on his face.

His smile immediately faltered, "Honey, you okay?"

Sandy looked up at him, yawning, "I didn't get much sleep last night. I kept waking up thinking about Micah."

Thomas knew Sandy, and her big heart was the thing that drew him to her. She deeply loves and cares for people.

"What you need is a hot cup of coffee!" Thomas said with a joking grin as he gave her a bear hug.

Sandy grabbed her purse and lab coat, and Thomas opened the door for her, offering his thoughts, "Sandy, I know you don't want to hear this, but you're going to see a lot of Micahs in your career. Somehow, you can't let yourself get so emotionally attached this quickly. I mean, you haven't even met him yet."

Closing the front door rather abruptly as they left, Sandy looked at Thomas, obviously irritated. Maybe it was her lack of sleep, but his words pierced right through her.

"I know that, Thomas, but that is one of the reasons I went to school to become a doctor in the first place. I want to be the type of physician that is compassionate and caring toward my patients. I don't want to be cold and just go through the motions. I want to care."

Thomas could tell that he had pushed the wrong button, and quickly made a peace offering. While waiting for the elevator, he grabbed Sandy's arm gently, leaned over, and stroked her long hair, "I'm sorry, honey. I shouldn't have been so harsh. Your heart is one of the many reasons why I love you. Not to mention your skills in the kitchen."

But Sandy was not in the mood for a joke, and she pulled away without the slightest hint of a smile. They barely spoke as they made their way to the car. Thomas started the car, backed out of the parking spot, and headed towards the hospital. He wished he could take all of it back. More importantly, he wished he could help.

Slowly, he glanced over at Sandy, "Please forgive me, Sandy. I should have been more understanding."

Sandy didn't say anything in response. Instead, she made a small, unhappy noise in her throat and stared out the window. Thomas thought about how many days he had until the major decision had to be made. He knew that it was not the time to bring it up, but he wished he could. It needed to be talked about.

They pulled up to the front entrance of the hospital. Having had enough time to cool down, Sandy leaned over and gave Thomas a quick peck on the cheek and wished him a good day.

"I love you, Sandy," Thomas said as she stepped out of the car.

Sandy turned, looking into his eyes, "Thomas, we have to make a decision, let's talk tonight. And ... I love you, too."

Sandy closed the door and began walking into the clinic. Pausing, she looked back to blow a quick kiss as Thomas pulled away from the curb.

Sandy knew the next few weeks of training were going to be trying. Before she passed through the hospital doors, she offered a quick prayer, "Lord, please help me, and lead me."

For her residency, Sandy would be working in the children's oncology unit. Each member of her team would be assigned to a patient. They would spend the day observing, reading their medical charts, and going on rounds with the attending physicians. Today, for the first time, the medical students all gathered at the nurses' station in anticipation of their new assignments.

Dr. Burns quickly handed out their folders, explaining how the clinical rotation would work.

"You will meet some very sick children during your

clinicals," he said. "It is best that you go in with a smile and a positive attitude."

He looked at them intently and continued, "Do not take anything personally. These parents carry a huge burden. Show them that you understand and want to help, but don't overwhelm them. We will meet back here at noon."

Sandy looked inside the folder she had been given and observed the same face she had seen yesterday, and all night in her dreams. She had been assigned to take care of Micah! Smiling to herself, she thought, *Thank you, Lord.*

Sandy had not seen Micah's mom yet that morning, but she knew it was still early. She made her way down the hallway to find Micah's room. As she walked in, a nurse was administering medication through his IV. Maggie, his mom, was sleeping in one of those uncomfortable hospital recliners, leaning toward the bed right next to Micah's head. Her arm was draped over his frail body. Sandy's heart suddenly ached with a deep sadness.

The nurse looked up as Sandy entered. She smiled, offering a good morning.

"Hello, I'm Sandy, the student resident doctor. How is the patient today?" she whispered, not wanting to wake up either of the sleeping family.

The nurse gave her a concerned look.

"He has had a rather rough night," she explained, "Yesterday, he had another round of chemo."

Sandy looked at Micah, sleeping so restfully. *What a*

beautiful child he is, she thought. *Fair skin, dark eyebrows, but no hair anymore. That's a shame. I can only imagine that at one time he had thick black hair that matched those soft eyebrows.*

Maggie slowly picked up her head, blinking up at Sandy, notably tired. "I remember you," she said, smiling.

"Yes, good morning. I am assigned to Micah today. I am glad you remember me," Sandy said, her voice still low.

"I must look horrible. I stayed up most of the night. Micah wasn't feeling well," she explained. She got up, stretched, and offered to get Sandy some coffee. "If you don't mind, would you sit with Micah?" she asked. "He has been vomiting all night, and I'd appreciate it if you stayed with him, just in case he wakes up. I don't want him to think I have left him alone."

"Of course, take your time. I'm sure you need a break. Maybe you can eat some breakfast. I'll stay right here."

Sandy pulled up a chair next to Micah's bedside and began looking through his chart while he was sleeping. Micah had been through three rounds of chemotherapy so far. Scanning the pages, Sandy thought, *This is such a hard ordeal to go through for such a young one.*

Sandy felt a slight tap on the chart and realized that Micah had awakened. She looked up to see those big brown eyes staring right at her.

"Hi. My name is Micah. Who are you?"

Micah's tone was one of curiosity and interest, not fear, and it made Sandy's heart melt a little bit.

"Hi, Micah. My name is Sandy. Your mom asked me

to sit with you so she could go eat some breakfast. I am a student resident doctor here, and I am very happy to meet you."

He frowned a little, not seeming as thrilled about this as Sandy was.

"So you're not really a real doctor, then?" Micah asked smartly.

Sandy couldn't help but giggle a little, "No, not all the way. I am still learning."

He didn't look particularly convinced, so Sandy changed the subject, noting the grey color of his skin and the dark circles under his big brown eyes, "I heard you had kind of a rough night last night."

"Yea … I had to have another round of bug juice."

"Bug juice?" Sandy asked, laughing.

"That's what I call it," Micah said with a slight smile. "What did you say your name was again?"

"Sandy."

"So how long are you going to stay here with me?" he asked.

"Well, we have different rotations, but each rotation is a few weeks, so I think I will be here for at least five or six weeks. Is that okay with you?"

"I guess that will be okay. It just seems like my doctors don't stay around here very long before they leave."

He paused for a moment, looking down at his hands, then looked back up, smiling, "Do you play cards? I play a mean game of rummy. Do you?"

"I love rummy! I don't think I have time to play right

now, but next time, maybe we can play a game. I mean, if you want," Sandy said with a smile.

"Absolutely!" Micah said, much more excited now than he had been only moments before.

"It's a date, then!" Sandy said, laughing.

Sandy noticed a laptop computer lying beside the bed and, out of curiosity, asked, "So, what's the computer for?"

With a big grin, Micah told Sandy, "I use it to talk to my friends on Facebook. My friends want to know how I'm doing, but my mom won't let me have a cell phone."

"How many friends do you have?" Sandy asked.

"I have over two thousand right now, and growing! They're from all over the place!" he said proudly.

"That's quite impressive, young man. I only have about forty-five! How did you make so many friends?"

Micah went on to explain that his friends at school told their friends about him, and they told others, and it just kept on going.

"Mitchell Thompson is my friend, too. And he is always checking up on me."

"Who is Mitchell Thompson?" asked Sandy.

Micah practically gasped in surprise, "You don't know Mitchell Thompson? Wow! He is only the best outfielder in baseball and plays centerfield with the St. Louis Cardinals! He comes to the hospital with some of the other players and visits us kids to cheer us up! He always comes to see me and makes me feel special. He calls me 'Superman'!"

Sandy smiled, "Hopefully, I'll get to meet your friends one day. For now, I think I'll send you an invitation to become my friend. Is that okay?"

Micah nodded, still smiling.

Sandy needed to finish reading his chart, but right then Maggie came back in from the cafeteria with a large mug of coffee in hand.

"Hi, my sweetheart," she said, leaning over to give Micah a kiss on the forehead. "How are you feeling?"

"Hi, Mom. I'm okay. Did you meet Sandy, my new doctor?"

Maggie gave Micah a quick wink.

"I have. I hope you haven't been talking her ears off!" she said, gently stroking Micah's face.

"I just told her about the bug juice and all my friends on Facebook! Sandy is going to play some rummy with me soon!"

"That's great. You know, Sandy, once he has you, he won't let you go. He will want you to play non-stop!"

For some reason, Maggie felt comfortable around Sandy, as if they had known each other for many years. She wondered if they were kindred spirits of a sort.

"I actually look forward to it," Sandy said, still smiling. "I will see you two in just a bit."

Holding tight to Micah's chart, Sandy offered a few farewells before heading to the lounge to sit down with some coffee of her own. She wanted to continue to learn about Micah and his medical condition. After a long morning, a hot cup of coffee was exactly what she needed. As she read, she quickly realized that Micah was much more ill than she had thought.

A tumor had been found six months ago after an accident during football. Surgeons had removed the tumor, hoping that it had not spread to other parts of his body. Sadly, the cancer traveled very quickly, and despite their hopes, tumors had continued to spread through his body. He was now in Stage Four, and there was not much else that could be done. Micah was in desperate need of a miracle.

Suddenly, Sandy began to feel sick to her stomach. "Lord you have to do something for this young boy," she prayed. "There is nothing worse than reaching a point of helplessness."

Before the shift was over, Sandy took her iPhone, logged on to Facebook, and sent a request to Micah to become friends. Around four-thirty, she called Thomas, and they discussed how mentally and physically exhausting a day it had been for both of them.

As the day came to a close, all they wanted to do was relax. "Please no shopping or bouncing around town tonight," Thomas told her, half joking.

Since they had promised to see each other and needed to talk, they decided to keep dinner simple. There was nothing like eating a grilled cheese sandwich and some hot tomato soup at Sandy's place. After a few minutes of peace and quiet, Thomas looked across the table at Sandy and told her what he had decided—she should not leave her residency.

She smiled and reached for Thomas's hand, "I was going to say the same thing to you."

The conversation slowly faded into the night, never really coming closer to really making a decision together. Someone had to step up to the plate and make the decision, but they both continued to 'agree to disagree,' and it didn't seem like either one of them would be putting their foot down any time soon.

Chapter Five

✳

The Decision

Thomas knew the day would come when he had to make up his mind and tell Mr. Danforth his decision. After pondering all night, it seemed they had three options. As he got ready for work, he thought through all of them.

The first and most preferred option is to get married, refuse to go to China, and pray they will let me keep my job, maybe in another capacity.

The second option is to still get married, but for Sandy to leave her residency and follow me to China.

The third option is for me to go to China and Sandy to stay in St. Louis to finish her residency.

Thomas appealed to God once again, "Father, please help me. Tell me what to do. I need an answer!"

Frustrated with his uncertainty, Thomas decided that he would take the chance and ask Mr. Danforth if there was any way that he could stay here and work in St. Louis for at least another year or so. Thomas called the office and asked Alice, Mr. Danforth's secretary, if she could make an appointment for him that afternoon. He could not put if off one more day.

After placing him on hold for a couple of minutes, Alice informed him, "Mr. Mitchell, Mr. Danforth said for you to meet him in Conference Room One at three o'clock, directly after the staff meeting. He has to leave a little early this afternoon."

Thomas agreed to the time and realized that he had not heard from Sandy all day. He texted her, letting her know his plan of attack with Mr. Danforth.

A few minutes later, the phone rang. It was Sandy.

"Thomas, are you sure?" she asked, "I'm a little concerned because we haven't talked about this completely!"

"I know, honey. Don't worry. Let's just put it in God's hands and see what happens. It can't hurt to ask, now can it?" Thomas asked, trying not to show how nervous he actually was.

"Okay, but call me as soon as the meeting is over. I want to hear every detail. I love you, Thomas!"

"I love you, too," he said, hanging up the phone. He could only hope that the words would come easily, and Mr. Danforth would listen with an open heart.

Thomas rushed over to Mr. Danforth's office a few minutes early and sat on the leather sofa outside the conference room. He felt like a kid again, as if he had been called into the principal's office for bad behavior. His heart pounded in his chest, and he was finding it difficult to keep his emotions in check. Beads of sweat spread across the bridge of his nose. He closed his eyes and begged God to give him the right words.

He had worked hard to get this dream position, but in one moment, it could all go up in smoke. On the other hand, Thomas felt he needed to draw from his faith, believing in "the substance of things hoped for and the evidence of things unseen." Thomas whispered to himself, *Come on faith … you can kick in any time now. Holy Spirit, I need you!*

Thomas noticed Alice looking directly at him over the top of her reading glasses. She offered Thomas a reassuring smile, which helped calm his nerves just a little bit.

"Are you nervous, Mr. Mitchell?" she asked with that small smile.

"Uh, yes, ma'am. Just a bit. Does it show?"

"Well, the constant tapping of your foot on the floor is a pretty good indicator. Don't worry. I've seen many things in my eight years behind this desk, but Mr. Danforth is a good man who listens and cares about his employees."

In spite of this reassurance, Thomas's foot began to tap even louder. Alice glanced at him again, a look of pity on her face. Blushing, Thomas froze and stopped his anxious foot. "I'm so sorry," he said with a sheepish grin.

Before she could respond, the phone rang. She answered it quickly, "Sir? Yes, sir. I will send him in."

She looked over at Thomas with another smile, "Mr. Mitchell, please follow me."

As staff members emptied out of the conference room, Thomas followed Alice through the door. He remembered that this particular conference room was used for new employee orientation. It looked much bigger now. A massive oak conference table with a thick glass top consumed the room. Plush, high-back leather chairs encircled the huge table.

Thomas thought about his last meeting with Mr. Danforth. *He offered me the job of a lifetime. Today, I may be walking away from it.*

The conference room was located directly beside Mr. Danforth's office. The large wooden door on the other side of the room was cracked open, and Thomas could see into the luxurious office. Alice led Thomas to the door, tapped lightly, and motioned for him to go in.

Mr. Danforth was seated behind his bulky desk, his chair turned to face the window. All of the window shades were drawn except for the one he faced. The bright afternoon sun was lighting up the room. Thomas could see the top of Mr. Danforth's head over the top of the chair. He could only imagine the stress Mr. Danforth encountered on a daily basis. He had a feeling this may not be a good day to have this conversation.

Not wanting to disrupt his thoughts, Thomas spoke quietly, "Mr. Danforth?"

When he still didn't react, Thomas was unsure if Mr. Danforth could even hear him. He called out his name again. This time he appeared to snap out of it, his head shaking a little.

Mr. Danforth turned around in his chair slowly. His eyes were red and glassy. He seemed to realize suddenly that he was not alone in the room and quickly wiped his eyes with a clean white handkerchief.

"I'm sorry to interrupt, Mr. Danforth. If it's not a good time, I can come back later," Thomas said, attempting to make the situation less uncomfortable.

"No, no, Mr. Mitchell. I'm terribly sorry. Please, sit down."

Thomas sat awkwardly in the overstuffed leather chair directly in front of the desk.

"These allergies are really getting to me today," Mr. Danforth said, wiping at his eyes again. "Mr. Mitchell, let me ask you a question, if I may. Have you ever felt so small and insignificant in this world we live in that you feel nothing matters because you do not have the power to change anything. That's how I sometimes feel in those conference meetings."

Thomas felt even more nervous, thinking Mr. Danforth might be speaking about him going to China and was about to drop the bad news in his lap. Perhaps he would tell him he didn't have a choice or that they didn't want him after all. Mr. Danforth appeared slightly depressed and probably wasn't feeling well. He didn't look like the man who had congratulated Thomas almost two weeks before.

Mr. Danforth continued without giving him a chance to answer the first deep and disconcerting question.

"Mr. Mitchell, do you have kids?" he asked suddenly,

catching Thomas off guard.

Thomas began to stutter, "Uh, n-no. No, not yet. But my fiancé and I hope to h-have children one day, God … God willing."

Thomas cleared his throat. He realized that he had not stuttered since he was a young boy. This meeting was making him extremely uncomfortable and the questions were suddenly making him feel like he was on trial. Mr. Danforth stared directly at Thomas, making him squirm in the over-stuffed chair.

Mr. Danforth leaned forward over his desk and looked at Thomas with an intense glare. "You just said 'God willing.' I take it you are a man of faith? That you believe in God?"

Thomas clenched his fists, unsure, as he thought about the question and Mr. Danforth's strange reaction. This is the head of one of the most prestigious companies in the United States, and he is asking me if I believe in God! I think I might have just blown it! Maybe he is an unbeliever, an agnostic, or an atheist! What if I say the wrong thing? But I can't lie! I have to be true to my Lord.

Thomas quickly dismissed his doubts and looked at Mr. Danforth, trying his best to be bold in his faith, "Yes, sir. Yes, I do!"

With a surge of sudden confidence, he continued to explain, "I have a deep faith in God. He is everything to me, sir!"

Mr. Danforth leaned back in his chair, folded his arms, and looked past Thomas as if deep in thought. He appeared to be contemplating what Thomas had just said. Thomas was thankful for the silence that gave him a moment to collect his thoughts.

Thomas did not always understand the complexities of life, but he knew that the realities of this world are not always compatible with the things of God. Mr. Danforth seemed to be having some deep thoughts about God at that moment, and it seemed as if Thomas had become his philosophical sparring partner for the time. Besides André, Thomas had never really talked about God at work. He always had an open Bible on his desk, and the frame holding a photo of Sandy said "God bless my family," but it rarely came up in conversation. Regardless, this meeting was not at all what Thomas had expected.

Mr. Danforth leaned forward again and threw out another question, "What do you do when your faith is shaken, Mr. Mitchell?"

Before Thomas could respond, the phone rang.

Mr. Danforth's countenance suddenly changed, deepening the lines on his forehead. His voice was shaky and not as deep and self-assured as usual.

"Yes ... I understand," he said into the receiver, nodding his head, "Okay ... I'm on my way!"

Noticeably upset, Mr. Danforth excused himself and rushed out of the office, leaving Thomas alone and a little stunned. He blinked, staring at the empty seat in front of him, trying to understand what had just happened.

Slowly, he stood and walked back through the main door. He looked at Alice who whispered an apology and offered an excuse for Mr. Danforth's strange behavior.

"I'm very sorry, Mr. Mitchell," she said. "It has been a particularly rough day for Mr. Danforth. Maybe you can try again tomorrow. I'll call you."

Thomas gladly accepted the offer for another appointment but still left the office perplexed. *What could have upset Mr. Danforth enough to make him leave in such a rush?* he thought. Only God knows, I guess.

❋

Outside, Mr. Ted Danforth did not wait for his driver. Instead, he jumped into the black Cadillac and headed toward the hospital as fast as he could, ignoring red lights and speed limits as he went. He began to pray to God. He had abandoned God many years ago, and now it felt awkward and empty, but it was all he had left.

"Dear God," he mumbled, trying to focus on the road, "I vowed I would never pray to you again after losing so much. You took my beloved wife, then my son, and now you are taking my grandson. But here I am, begging you for my grandson's life. How do I say to let your will be done? How could I ever do that? I can't, God! I just can't! Not if it means his life! I have worked hard all my life, and I followed you closely for many years. Is this how you repay a faithful follower? By taking everything he loves? I don't understand! If you save Micah, I promise I will give you one more chance. I will change and do whatever you want me to do. I will give up every cent I own! Just … save him …"

Halfway to the hospital, he couldn't take it anymore. He pulled the car over to the side of the road. His tears blurred his vision, and he knew he had to find a way to pull himself together before he got there. He had to be strong for Micah and Maggie. For at least fifteen minutes, he sat there crying. Suddenly, there was a loud tap on the driver's window. He hadn't noticed the police car pulling up behind him, with blue lights now flashing in his rear view mirror. Slightly irritated, he rolled down his window, frowning up into the officer's eyes.

"Sir, are you okay?" asked the officer.

Wiping his tears away, he slammed his hand down hard on the edge of the steering wheel, "No, Officer, I am not okay!" he snapped, "My grandson is dying, and there is nothing I can do about it. Do you have any idea who I am? I can put a sleek, top-notch aircraft in the air, but I cannot do one thing to save my own grandson!"

As soon as the words flew out of his mouth, he felt ashamed and out of control.

But the officer reached through the open window and placed his hand on his shoulder. "Yes, sir," he said in a soft voice, "I do know who you are. I also believe that God puts people in our path for a reason, Mr. Danforth!"

Ted let his head fall forward onto the steering wheel, not even thinking about how the officer knew his name. "I don't know about God anymore, Officer. I used to believe in many things, but I have seen and been through too much. I'm afraid my faith in God has been shaken."

The officer continued to try to explain in a gentle

tone, "Sir, I do know who you are. Your emblem for the company is on your car, and everyone knows who you are in this town. You're Teddy Danforth! You kind of saved my life."

Looking up quickly, Ted's misery began to turn into annoyed anger as he glared at the officer once more, "What in the world does that have to do with anything? What are you talking about?"

The officer could tell that Mr. Danforth was very upset but continued to try to explain.

"A few years ago, I had a wife and son. They were in a tragic car crash. The medical bills had piled up, and the town took up a collection. I guess you read about it in the local newspaper. You came by the station and handed me a check. You paid off all our hospital bills. You even came by the hospital to visit them in ICU."

Caught off guard, Ted suddenly recognized the young police officer, "You're John McBride?"

"Yes, sir, I am," Officer McBride said, smiling. He was obviously a little relieved, hoping that Mr. Danforth's barriers were finally coming down. He figured he might even be able to help him.

Ted's face started to soften.

"So, how is the family? Happy? Healthy?" he asked.

"No, sir …" McBride said with a frown. "I'm afraid I lost both of them, sir. Brandon's head injuries were so bad that he never did wake up. My wife, Linda, well, she gave up once she knew Brandon was gone. She took her own life a couple of weeks later. You see, Mr. Danforth, I know pain, too."

Ted suddenly felt immense pain in his chest. He could not form the words he wanted to say.

"Oh, God," he groaned. "I am so sorry, I didn't know!"

With a sad smile, the officer continued to offer Mr. Danforth encouraging words.

"There is no way you could have known, Mr. Danforth," he said quietly. "But I do believe it was God who was with me the whole time, and He has been ever since. I cannot explain why bad things happen. We live in an imperfect world. I think our heavenly Father is shedding tears right along with us. But if we give Him the chance, He can cover our hurts with His love."

Mr. Danforth contemplated the officer's words. He was overwhelmed with sorrow for the man and still fighting his own pain inside, but he forced himself to offer his own thoughts, "So, instead of lashing out and blaming God, you are saying that I should let Him love me through this."

"Yes, sir," McBride said, smiling again, "that is exactly what I am saying."

Mr. Danforth extended his hand out through the open window to shake the officer's hand, "Thank you, Officer McBride. Thank you so much. And again, I am so sorry for your loss."

Officer McBride squeezed Mr. Danforth's hand, "Let me give you a police escort to see your grandson. I'm sure he needs you!"

Ted gave him a small smile of gratitude, still reeling from the whole encounter.

"Before we go, may I share one more thing?" asked Officer McBride.

Mr. Danforth paused, suddenly feeling that this was a moment of God, and who was he to interfere with God?

"Our God is a loving God who only wants the very best for us. We want the best for our children, do we not? A loving father would not make bad things happen to his children. When we hurt, they hurt. Just know, Mr. Danforth, that God loves you!"

Ted managed to give the officer a smile, "Thank you, sir. I needed to hear that today."

Chapter Six

✳

Calling Micah Home

Micah was having an especially rough day. His temperature kept spiking, and the nausea was getting worse. He continued to fall in and out of sleep, and as he dreamed, he could see himself in a sky full of clouds. He was light as a feather, jumping from cloud to cloud. Suddenly, the path of clouds ended, and there was only a door. As he stared at the door, he realized he had a decision to make. Should he turn around and jump back, or should he open the door? The answer came on its own, slipping through his thoughts, *I am not ready to walk through that door.* Taking a step back, he turned around and jumped back across the clouds until he was far away from the door and began to feel tired. With a sigh, he sat down on the last cloud and fell fast asleep.

Micah woke up slowly, realizing he was still in his

hospital bed. He turned to see his grandpa sitting by his bed. He could feel his grandpa's large, warm hand lying on his own.

"Hi, Grandpa," Micah said, his voice weak and strained.

"Hello, there, my strong boy. Did you have a good sleep?" Mr. Danforth said.

"Oh, Grandpa, I had the most wonderful dream. I was playing on top of the clouds, and I was so light! I didn't even hurt anymore," he said with a smile. Taking a deep breath, Micah continued, "There was a door, but I was afraid to open it, so I turned around and jumped back through the clouds until I got tired, and then I fell asleep."

"That is a fine dream. How are you feeling now?" asked Micah's grandfather with deep concern on his face.

Micah paused, and a frown settled over his soft, young face. "I don't want to tell Mom, but I am getting real tired, Grandpa. Can I ask you something? Well, I kind of asked you before, but you never did answer me."

Ted knew exactly what he was going to ask. It had been brought up a few times but was never answered, and he was still not ready. He thought to himself, *Okay, God, if You are there after all, then give me an answer to tell my grandson. I am begging you!*

Suddenly, he could hear a still, small voice resonate deep in his heart. It seemed to say, "Tell Micah I love him." He sat up in his chair in surprise, as if he had been hit directly on the back of his head. It was not an audible voice, but it was a felt one, and the message was clear, as if it had been whispered right next to him.

Officer McBride's words rang out through his thoughts once more, "God loves you."

He took hold of both of Micah's small hands and spoke softly to him before he could ask the question, "All I know, Micah, is that God loves you."

Micah sighed and smiled just a little bit and appeared to be satisfied with the answer. He slowly closed his eyes and whispered, "I knew it," as he fell asleep once again.

Sandy had spent most of the morning with Micah and his mom, until a change in schedule forced her to work elsewhere for a large chunk of the afternoon. At home, she had spent a lot of time studying the type of cancer that Micah was diagnosed as having, and she knew well that, at stage four, short of a miracle, the odds were not in Micah's favor. She wasn't sure how she could deal with such a hopeless situation and felt that the best she could do was stay by his and Maggie's side, offering what comfort and happiness she could.

After her shift, she decided to stop by to see Micah one more time before heading home. Maggie had gone home to shower and change clothes but said she would be back within the hour. Micah's mom was amazing. She had been a single mom since Micah was two years old. Micah was truly her whole life and represented all that was good in this world to her.

Sandy came around the corner just in time to see an older, well-dressed man coming out of Micah's room and heading off. Sandy peeked through the door into Micah's room, happy to find that he was awake.

"Sandy!" Micah called out, breaking into a big grin.

"Hi, buddy. I didn't want to wake you, but I can see you are awake already."

"Sandy, Grandpa came to see me!"

"I see that, did you have a nice visit?"

"Yes, but I feel sorry for him, Sandy," said Micah, his smile wilting. "He's really scared, I can tell. But I'm not scared!"

Not thinking, Sandy asked, "Scared of what?"

"Dying, of course!" Micah said, his mood unchanging.

Sandy felt like she was being torn inside out as she tried to be strong and not show how much pain she was feeling, "You're not scared?"

"Nope. There is this big door in the clouds. I've seen it! When I'm done jumping on all the clouds, I am going to open the door and walk right through," explained Micah, practically bursting with excitement.

Sandy stood amazed at the bravery of this young boy in the face of death. *If only I was this brave*, she thought to herself.

She could feel her heart beating fast, and tears were forming in her eyes. If she didn't leave soon, she knew she was going to lose it, and she really didn't want Micah to see her cry. She gave herself a quick pep talk, *Keep it together! For Micah!*

"Grandpa told me that God loves me, and I know that's who is behind the door. I just know it," said Micah, still smiling.

Sandy watched Micah carefully, gently stoking his head, "Your grandfather is a very wise man."

She knew she could not say too much about her beliefs. As a doctor, she had to be mindful not to express her own beliefs too strongly and to respect all faiths. But in her heart, she knew that God could heal, and He used many different people to do His work.

If the time presented itself, Sandy would be glad to tell Micah about the wonderful, loving God she knew, but her spirit warned that it was not the time. And it seemed that Micah had an idea of God's love already.

A bible verse ran through Sandy's mind as she prepared to leave Micah's side. She remembered that Jesus had said, *"Suffer little children, and forbid them not, to come to me: for of such is the kingdom of heaven."*

That story was one Sandy's mother had taught her, and it always stayed deep within her heart. Some had brought children to Jesus, but the disciples rebuked them. Sandy was not sure why. Maybe they thought they were too young to understand. But Jesus told his disciples to let them come. Micah was searching, and in Sandy's heart, she knew that God was showing Micah the way to Him.

Offering a smile, Sandy said, "Goodnight, Micah. God bless you."

"Night, Sandy! Do you mind if I give you a hug?" he asked with a sheepish grin.

"You certainly may!" she replied, smiling. She couldn't help it and thought to herself, *Professional or not, how do you turn down a hug?*

Afterward, Sandy called Thomas to let him know that she had finished her shift for the night. Thomas said he was already on his way to pick her up and would meet her outside the ER entrance. It was not more than a few minutes later when Thomas pulled up.

"Hi, babe," he said as she sat down.

Sandy could tell from his long face that the meeting may not have gone well. She looked at her phone, realizing with a groan that he had tried to call a couple times, and she had forgotten to call him back.

"I'm really sorry, honey. I was so busy today. I saw I had missed messages from you, but I just didn't have time to call."

"Don't worry. There is nothing to tell. Mr. Danforth had an emergency and flew out of the office before I could talk with him. We have another meeting set up for tomorrow. But you had a busy day, huh?"

Sandy began to tell Thomas about Micah and his dream. She could feel her voice quiver as she shared what Micah had said about God.

"Thomas, God is reaching out to him. I can feel it. I want so badly to tell him everything that is in my heart. But I'm not sure if his parents are believers in God, and if it is even my place as a resident doctor. They drill us so hard about not bringing our beliefs into a patient's room."

Thomas turned to Sandy and took her hand. "Sandy, have faith. When the time is right, it will come together. Sometimes we work so hard to make things happen, when it is not our job. Learning to trust in God, knowing in our spirit that God knows what He is doing is a very hard lesson to learn. Saying it is one thing, walking in it is another. Believe me, after today, I am not sure what God's game plan is for me. For us. I guess it just isn't time for us to know. And patience is a virtue, I'm told."

Sandy looked at Thomas, seeing a strong and intelligent man, full of faith. He always moved forward with such fervor. She knew that this trouble with work was hard on him, and she was sure that even if Thomas had doubts, he was not letting her see them right then. He was trying to be strong for her.

At her apartment, Thomas walked her to the door, kissed her, and pulled her into his arms for a much-needed hug.

"You know, Micah asked me to give him a hug goodbye today."

"Oh, he did, huh? I see I have a little competition, don't I?" Thomas said, laughing.

Sandy laughed as well, thinking about the sad, strong little boy and his bright smile.

"Did you give him one after all?" Thomas asked after a moment, knowing that it may go against hospital policy.

"Yep, I sure did," Sandy said with a smile. "He needed one, and I couldn't resist."

Thomas winked at her, "That's my girl!"

Chapter Seven

✳

The Intertwining

*M*aggie spoke into the phone, "Hi, Dad. It's me, Maggie! I was just checking on you. I must have just missed you at the hospital yesterday! Micah said you stopped by. Micah is so tired, Dad. I am doing okay, but I sure miss Tom. I know you do, too, Dad. You have been so wonderful to take care of Micah and me. He would be so happy to know you are with us. I am sorry this is such a short phone call, but we will talk later. I love you! Bye, Dad."

Maggie hung up the phone thinking she may have said too much in her message. Mr. Danforth still struggled with the death of his son, Tom, just like Maggie. Micah had only been two when Tom passed, and it was such a sudden death that it hit the family hard. The doctors said it was an aneurysm, and no one had seen it coming. He may have had the condition from birth, but they never knew it. While Tom did suffer from migraines as he got older, he never went to the doctor. It was like pulling teeth to get him to go. He always took a handful of Extra Strength Acetaminophen capsules to control the pain, but that would only last for a short time. And no one forced him to get checked out. Everyone believed it was stress related.

Throughout his life, Tom had worked alongside his dad at the company and assumed many of the executive-related activities so his father could enjoy full, sunny days at the golf course. Tom had the most wonderful mind. Maggie would even have called him a genius. He had actually developed many of the modern aircraft designs they were using today. He was a loving father and husband, too. Ted, whom Maggie often called 'Dad,' had really been like a father to her. Every time Ted looked at Micah, she was sure he was seeing Tom and all the possibilities of what could have been, and perhaps even what still could be if only Micah were well. So many times, Maggie worried that losing Micah would be something neither she nor Ted could handle. She wasn't sure they could handle losing someone all over again.

Maggie reflected back on when she first met Tom. It had been kind of a miracle that Tom and Maggie ever ended up together in the first place. Tom and his family were very involved in church, and Tom was raised in a very loving Christian home. In fact, Mr. Danforth had once been a deacon at their church. Maggie, on the other hand, had come from a broken home and certainly not a church-going family. She did not know much about God at all. All Maggie could remember from her adolescent years was the children's song, *Jesus Loves Me*.

Maggie had been working at a little coffee and donut shop in the city. Mr. Danforth and his family would come by before church almost every Sunday. Maggie was seventeen at the time and was always happy to wait on them because she knew they were really good tippers. But they were also very kind and always invited her to their church.

Maggie always thanked them but said the usual, "I have to work but maybe next time."

A couple of months passed where Maggie did not see them at all, and she wondered what had happened. One morning Mr. Danforth and Tom showed up. Mr. Danforth looked haggard and miserable. Maggie was sad to find out that Mrs. Danforth had passed away. She had been fighting pancreatic cancer for some time, but it had taken a turn for the worse, and she didn't make it.

Mr. Danforth introduced Maggie to Tom that day, and they became instant friends, despite his recent loss. They seemed to fall in love almost right away. The next time they visited and invited Maggie to church, she gladly accepted. Maggie had finally made that choice because of Tom, but it turned out that his family was the best thing that ever happened to her.

They took her under their wing, and before she knew it, Mr. Danforth was putting Maggie through college. He became the father she never had. Maggie's mom had done the best she could with what she had, but it was hard for her to raise four kids as a single mom, and it had never really worked out for their family.

Tom and Maggie started dating almost immediately, but the rules were very strict in his home, and Tom had great respect for his father. Their only differences were that Tom wanted to be a doctor, and Mr. Danforth wanted him to be an engineer. Out of respect for his dad's wishes, Tom decided to pursue a career in the aeronautical industry, just like his dad, and never complained. After losing his wife, Mr. Danforth unknowingly held onto Tom even harder, not wanting to lose him in any way.

Maggie finished college with a degree in Social Work, and Tom finished his degree in Engineering. They married quickly, and it was not long before Maggie was pregnant with Micah. With Micah's birth, you would have thought they had given Mr. Danforth the world. He was so happy, knowing he was having his first grandchild, and a boy at that.

After Ted's wife passed, he began to attend church less and less. There was always one excuse after another not to go. Then, after loosing Tom, he stopped going completely. Losing so much in such a short time seemed to have pushed him over the edge, and he felt he had no faith left to hold on to.

But Maggie always believed that Ted truly loved God and held onto the hope that he would find his way back to Him. She knew that God would always understand and love him, and she never stopped praying for him.

Maggie knew the feeling of wanting to quit: to just

give in to the pain and give up. Sometimes she wondered how she was going to make it, too. At one point, Maggie had to quit her job at CPS because the stress proved too much for her. She could not take care of Micah and handle the stresses of her job at the same time, all while missing her husband. Even through his own pain, Mr. Danforth had managed to be a constant source of support for Maggie through this time.

That afternoon, Thomas was still thinking about the plans that God had for Sandy and him. He prayed once more for a productive meeting. He proceeded to his appointment with Mr. Danforth, this time back in his office. He was hoping that he could finally get some answers about going to China.

After checking in with the secretary he sat down on the long, black leather sofa once again. *This time*, he told himself, *I will stay calm and relaxed*. Thomas thought about their last conversation, still uncertain about Mr. Danforth and the reasons for his strange line of questioning.

It seemed only minutes before Thomas was ushered into Mr. Danforth's office. This time, Mr. Danforth was not sitting down but standing near the door as if he had been waiting for Thomas to enter. He stepped forward and offered a handshake before gesturing toward a small mahogany table on the other side of the office near the far window. They sat down, and Thomas expected Mr. Danforth to sit on one end and him at the other. Instead, Mr. Danforth sat down right next to Thomas, turning to face him. He was almost too close for Thomas to be comfortable.

"Hello, Mr. Mitchell. First, let me apologize for running out on you yesterday. It was, well, something that could not be helped," Mr. Danforth explained.

"Please, sir, no apology is necessary," Thomas stammered, still trying to relax. "That is perfectly fine, really. Sometimes things just happen."

"So, what can I do for you, Mr. Mitchell?" Mr. Danforth took a deep breath, watching Thomas carefully. "Before you answer, though … may I say that you look like someone that I held, and still do hold, very close to my heart."

Thomas was taken aback and completely unsure of where this was going, and he was a little afraid that this might be a repeat performance of the last meeting. He took a moment to reply, "Really, sir? Who might that be?"

"My son Tom. He … well, he passed away about ten years ago, but there is not a day that goes by that I do not think of him," Mr. Danforth said, taking another long, deep breath.

"I am so sorry for your loss, sir. I can't imagine how hard that must have been."

Thomas felt that he should say more, but the words suddenly escaped him.

"Okay, well, enough about my life and its problems. As I said, what can I do for you, Mr. Mitchell?"

Sandy had been such a tremendous support as she had listened intently to Thomas rehearsing this speech repeatedly over the last few days. He had finally reached a point where he felt comfortable with what he wanted to say and how, but now that the time had arrived, it felt like he had cotton in his mouth. Thomas prayed silently to himself, *Please, Lord ... Let the words come freely.*

"Mr. Danforth, first let me say what an honor it is to work for your company," Thomas began. "I cannot tell you how much I enjoy working here. I feel I am a part of this family, and have learned a great deal from my coworkers. There is no doubt that I want to take the position you've offered me, but I have some concerns about going to China right now. I'm sure it's a great challenge, and I can do the job well, but, but…"

Thomas's words tapered off. Mr. Danforth had gotten up from the table and moved to sit behind his large desk. He clasped his hands, looking intently at Thomas with a stare that penetrated right through him.

"I am listening, Mr. Mitchell."

"Sir, would you mind if I stand?"

"By all means, Mr. Mitchell."

Thomas got up and stood in front of his desk. It was difficult to look directly at his boss's face at that moment. Mr. Danforth had this way about him that made Thomas feel almost incapable of approaching him.

"Sir, my fiancé has worked very hard to get into medical school here and is now working on her residency. She won't be done with her training for a couple years. That means that, for this position, either she will have to give up everything she has worked so hard for to go with me, or we will have to be separated for two years, at least. That is something I am not sure I can cope with, Mr. Danforth. Life is too short. Now, if you do not mind, I would like to ask you a question?"

Mr. Danforth nodded.

"Have you ever had a wonderful blessing that at the same time felt like it was a curse? I am extremely grateful for this opportunity, but it has also been such a burden on both of our hearts, and I'm not sure I can take the position in China if it means this kind of strife for us. I hope you understand."

Mr. Danforth leaned forward, placing the weight of his crossed arms over the desk, still looking directly at Thomas.

"Mr. Mitchell," he said, his eyes never leaving Thomas's face, "I truly understand about life being too short."

He paused, looking down at his clenched fists, "In fact, I recently learned ... well, never mind all that. I will have to do some thinking about this, Mr. Mitchell. We were really counting on you representing our company in China. Your supervisor has given you the highest recommendation for this position, but at the same time we do not want to lose you either. Give me a couple days to mull this over, look at some options, and we will meet again."

Thomas could not ask for more. Mr. Danforth had not dismissed his concerns altogether, nor had he shown him the door.

Unable to contain his grin, he shook Mr. Danforth's hand firmly, saying, "Thank you, Mr. Danforth, for your time and consideration. I look forward to meeting with you again."

Thomas left Mr. Danforth's office feeling a little relieved, but also knowing that at this point the whole situation was in God's hands. While walking back to his own workspace, he felt that God was calling to him, telling him to let Him hold the situation in His hands, rather than Thomas's.

As promised, Thomas called Sandy to fill her in on the results of the meeting. Afterward, she mentioned that it was Micah's birthday and that they would be having a small party in his room that afternoon. She asked if Thomas could pick up a gift and come by later. He agreed without hesitation. He had never met Micah before and looked forward to stepping into Sandy's world and away from his own.

"Sure, honey. How old is Micah again?

"He will be turning thirteen, and I know he loves games. But I think I will leave that up to you."

"Okay, that won't be a problem."

"See you later, then. Love you," Sandy said, hanging up quickly.

Thomas made his way to the nearest electronics store to find a game that he thought Micah would enjoy. Old memories came back to life as he noticed a hand-held chess game. He could still recall his own father teaching him how to play chess so many years ago.

He used to say to Thomas, "Every boy needs to learn to play chess. It is a game about life. It is full of strategies, smarts, and skill. If you can play chess, you can play anything."

It didn't take much more than that memory for him to decide what to buy. Leaving the store, Thomas made one more stop, choosing to buy a regular chessboard instead. He had always felt that some things are just better when they are hands-on. It had been a long time since Thomas had played, but he thought he might be able to teach Micah, just like his father taught him.

Sandy had spent the morning with Maggie decorating Micah's room. He wanted to help, but Sandy continued insisting he get some rest before the party.

"Hey, Micah," Sandy said, smiling, after she hung up the phone. "Guess what? My boyfriend is coming to your party! His name is Thomas."

"What? I thought I was your only boyfriend!" Micah said with a fake scowl. He couldn't hold it and quickly burst into a large, heart-melting grin.

While patting Micah on the head, Sandy said, "Shhhh, don't tell Thomas. He may get jealous!"

"Hey, what's all this laughing going on in here?" asked Maggie as she came in carrying more bags of goodies. "You would think there was a party going on."

Sandy helped Maggie put the bags on the table they had set up on the far side of the small room.

Micah looked up at them, "Mom, Sandy's boyfriend, Thomas, is coming!"

"That's great, Sandy! I've wanted to meet him," said

Maggie as she unpacked the party supplies.

Over the past couple of weeks, Maggie and Sandy had gotten to know each other fairly well. When two people spend hours and days together, there are parts of their life they cannot resist sharing. Maggie had confided to Sandy about Tom, her husband, and his unexpected passing. She was particularly proud of the way that Tom had made God the center of their family. As Micah's parents, they raised Micah to understand who God is and what He has done for us, keeping it simple so he could understand at such a young age. When Tom died, her faith certainly had been shaken, but somehow she was still able to trust God and go on. But Micah's sickness had pushed Maggie once more to a place of desperation.

Sandy remembered Maggie saying to her, only the other day, "How can a loving God take our children and allow sicknesses to come on them?"

It was something Sandy had pondered many times throughout medical school, but all she could do was offer her own thoughts, "Maggie, God loves you and Micah. We live in a world where we don't have the answers, and that is why we must look to God for solutions. Our bodies fail us, just as people fail us. We can only pray for Him to continue to be with Micah and give you the faith and strength to get through this, no matter how long it takes."

She knew in her heart that the words were not going to offer much comfort. Here was a mother watching her son slowly dying. There were no words that could take away that pain. She felt helpless and the only thing left was to pray for a miracle.

Sandy helped Maggie decorate the room with streamers and balloons, as Micah directed their every move. He was quite the taskmaster.

As Sandy hung the last balloon, she heard Micah call out, "Grandpa!"

Turning around, Sandy saw the same well-dressed man who had left Micah's room the day before. He was an imposing figure, but it was thrown off a little by the large, brightly-colored birthday bag he was carrying.

"Hi, Dad," said Maggie, walking over to give him a hug. "Dad, this is Sandy, she is—"

"She's my doctor!" interrupted Micah, smiling from ear to ear.

"Hello, Sandy. My name is Ted. Nice to meet you!"

"Grandpa, she is my girlfriend, but her boyfriend doesn't know yet! We plan to break the news to him today!" Micah said, laughing hysterically.

"Micah!" scolded Maggie, but she was laughing, too. "You are a little prankster!"

Just then, Thomas walked into the laughter-filled room. "Hi, everybody," he said with a smile. "Did I miss the party?"

Mr. Ted Danforth turned around to see who had just entered his grandson's room. Thomas's mouth fell open, and both men stood staring at each other in surprise and disbelief.

Was this encounter a coincidence? Or are we looking at God's playbook? Only time will tell.

Chapter Eight

❋

Surprise Meeting

t took a moment for Maggie, Sandy, and Micah's laughter to die down before they noticed the surprised looks of the two men.

"Are we missing something here?" asked Maggie, watching them with a confused frown.

After recovering from unexpectedly finding his boss in the room, Thomas smiled and offering him a handshake.

"Well, it appears to be a small world after all, does it not, Mr. Mitchell?" Ted said, shaking his hand.

"It appears that way, sir," he turned toward Sandy. "Mr. Danforth, have you met my fiancée, Doctor Sandy Fogel, yet?"

"I have only just met the doctor, Mr. Mitchell, and I was unaware she was the fiancée you spoke of earlier."

Sandy took a step forward and shook Mr. Danforth's hand, "It's nice to officially meet you, sir. Thomas has told me a lot about you."

"All good, I hope!" Ted said with a smile. Looking down at Micah, Mr. Danforth gave him a wink, "Micah, I have some bad news. Your girlfriend is an engaged woman."

Micah, with his quick wit, replied, "Yeah, well, you know, Grandpa, you win some and you lose some."

Everyone burst into laughter.

"Sandy," Mr. Danforth said, "my daughter-in-law has spoken very highly of you. And from what I can see, you have been very good medicine for my grandson."

Sandy, still feeling slightly intimidated, tried her best to smile, "It's my pleasure sir. And, really, he makes my job easy."

Mr. Danforth turned to Thomas and gave him a strong pat on the back. "I know about this young man already. We are very lucky to have him with us as well."

The excitement seemed to be a little much for Micah, as he got very quiet and laid his head back down on his pillow. Sometimes he seemed to get little bursts of energy that almost made one think he was not sick at all, but then the weakness would return. It brought the whole group back to reality, remembering with sadness that Micah was still a fragile, sick young man who was fighting for his very life.

Maggie looked over as she noticed Micah's sudden exhaustion, "Micah, are you okay?"

Micah was not going to miss his party and managed a smile, but he wouldn't admit that he was getting tired.

"Sorry, mom," he said, trying to make his mood lift

again. "I am just getting sleepy. Maybe we should cut the cake now."

Everyone gathered around his bed, and several nurses on the floor stopped by to sing "Happy Birthday" to Micah with the group.

Thomas laid his gift beside him on the bed, "Sandy and I thought you might like this."

Micah slowly opened the present, relishing the moment, and was genuinely surprised when he saw his gift. "A chess set!" he said with a sudden burst of excited energy.

He didn't even notice the second gift: an electronic game that lay at the bottom of the bag.

"How did you know, Mr. Thomas?" he asked in delight. "Grandpa, we can play chess here at the hospital now!"

Micah looked at Thomas again, "Grandpa and I used to play chess all the time. He has this big chess set, but it is too heavy to bring here, so this is perfect. We can play right now if you want to!"

Thomas looked over at Mr. Danforth who was wiping his eyes with his handkerchief. "I would say a game is in order if Micah is up to it."

"Yes, indeed!" replied Mr. Danforth.

Micah looked at Maggie, hoping for her approval. Maggie smiled, but warned, "If you feel like it, Micah. But there is always tomorrow if you don't."

Micah looked over at Sandy, who was smiling but trying not to cry, their thoughts almost identical. Both of them were thinking that tomorrow was not promised to any of us, and what if tomorrow never came? In the twinkling of an eye, Micah could be jumping from cloud to cloud for the last time, finally opening heaven's door to step inside for all eternity.

Sandy moved to the bedside table near Micah as Thomas took the chess set out of its box. He carefully set up the pieces, one by one, on the table. Mr. Danforth moved closer, watching every movement, as if everything was moving in slow motion. Observing Thomas putting the pieces in order on the board, he was aware that something in his heart was telling him this might be the last game he would ever play with his grandson.

He looked down at Micah, picturing his son Tom when he was a young boy. Micah looked so much like his father. Then he looked over at Thomas who resembled his son quite a bit as well. Memories flashed before him of the many times they had played chess together.

Maggie sat down in a chair by the window, trying to hold in her emotions. The laughter had brought such a sweet release, but it also opened up the wound in her heart that had yet to heal. As she closed her eyes slowly, she was oblivious to what was happening around her. How could she say goodbye? How could she not become a bitter woman after all of this? What did she ever do to deserve losing her husband and now her son? The thoughts engulfed her mind in a roaring flood.

From beside the bed, Sandy looked up to see Maggie sitting by the window all alone. She could see the grief on Maggie's face. It was a picture of helplessness that Sandy had not witnessed before on her strong, determined face. Sandy thought to herself, *what a horrible place to be: where there is no place to run or hide.*

Maggie was an amazing mother and had tried never to let Micah see her sadness. What she didn't know was that Micah had always been observant and noticed far more than she realized. He worried about her, as well. Sandy felt in her heart that she should go to her but was unsure. *What can I say that will provide any comfort?*

Taking a deep breath, Sandy walked slowly over to Maggie and pulled up a chair next to her. Without saying anything, she put her arms around the strong, grieving mother.

Maggie looked up, her lips quivering, and whispered, "I don't think I can take this much longer, Sandy. I can see my Micah slowly slipping away."

Looking into Maggie's tear-filled eyes, Sandy whispered a verse into her ear as it came to her heart, *"I will lift up mine eyes unto the hills, from whence cometh my help. My help comes from the Lord, which made heaven and earth."*

Sandy could barely get the words out, as her own emotions threatened to overwhelm her, and she knew she was very close to breaking down and crying as well.

Maggie looked at Sandy and began to talk about her fears. They were things she never really wanted to admit, even to herself, "Sandy, I know that our days are numbered. I realize that I may have to say goodbye any day now. I have begged God to save my son, but each day he gets sicker and sicker. It is so difficult to keep the faith and believe that God will heal my Micah, when just the opposite seems to be happening. I feel God's presence every time I look at Micah and hear the peace in his voice. But at the same time, when I ask God to heal my son, I feel selfish because I want to hold onto him as long as I possibly can."

Sandy looked at Maggie and could not seem to provide an answer for her or words to comfort her. All she could do was to be there for her and Micah when they needed her most. That was all the comfort and support she felt she could provide.

Maggie grabbed Sandy's hands suddenly and squeezed them, whispering, "Thank you, Sandy."

Wiping her eyes and putting on a smile, Maggie slowly stood, and walked over to Micah.

"So, who is winning the game?" she asked.

Thomas spoke up and said, "I think this is going to be anyone's guess."

"Grandpa, you better not let me win, or I'll be mad!"

Mr. Danforth offered a quick response, "Your game has really improved. I think you must have had a very good instructor!"

"Grandpa, you know you taught me everything I know!" said Micah, smiling.

Not really thinking about chess, Mr. Danforth thought to himself, *so little time. Did I really show him everything he needed to know in his young life.*

The game finally ended with Micah pulling out the victory. He had played his heart out. Thomas collected the pieces and the chessboard and placed them neatly back into the box.

It had been a long game, and Micah was very tired. After closing his eyes, he laid his head back on his pillow. Speaking with his eyes closed, Micah said, "Thank you Mom, Grandpa, Sandy, and Mr. Thomas, for such a great party. I think I am going to sleep now."

The group of them gazed at Micah and, in unison, said, "Goodnight, Micah," quietly and offered one more "Happy Birthday." After a few moments, Thomas and Sandy left to go home, leaving Maggie and Mr. Danforth sitting with Micah. Sandy looked back once more at the beautiful boy lying in the bed.

"Father … is it ever too late to pray for a miracle?"

Micah drifted off to sleep and began to dream of clouds. As they watched, Maggie and Mr. Danforth noticed the smile that had come across Micah's face. He was somewhere else, somewhere happy. Not here.

Micah jumped once again from cloud to cloud, feeling light as a feather, just as before. Soon he came to the door at the end of the clouds. It was a large door and felt warm and inviting. This time, the door was ajar. He felt compelled to walk through it and was sure he would be glad when he did.

He looked back and could see that it was a long way back across the clouds. Thinking about it, he knew he was too tired to turn back, so he reached for the handle and pushed the door wide open. Without hesitation, he stepped through the entrance, and there was no turning back. Micah was finally home in the presence of Jesus.

Sandy went to bed with an incredible heaviness in her heart. Throughout the night, she had an unusual urge to check her Facebook page. This had never happened before, and the impulse was quite strong. What could it be, she thought as she pulled herself out of bed and headed to her computer. As Sandy opened her page, she found a message from Micah that had been sent that afternoon.

With a sudden sense of panic, Sandy began to read, "To all my FB friends, I won't be here tomorrow. But please don't be sad for me because I know I'll be in Heaven tonight. Thank you for supporting me and giving me the courage to fight. Mom and Grandpa, thank you for loving me and always being by my side. I love you very much. I know that one day we will see each other again. Sandy, don't ever give up hope for other kids just like me. Micah."

As soon as Sandy had finished reading Micah's name, tears already in her eyes, the phone rang. Glancing over at the clock, she numbly wondered who would call at one o'clock in the morning. Wiping at her tears, she answered the phone. It was Maggie, whimpering. Not able to contain her sorrow, Sandy's tears flowed faster as she heard Maggie begging on the line.

"Sandy, he's gone. Please come over. I need you!"

Throwing on some jeans, she called Thomas and explained. He promised to be right over.

Sandy began to cry, "Oh God, I know You love Micah and Maggie, and I am not trying to question You, but Father, this is hard … I don't know if I am made to be a doctor. How can I face this day in and day out? The feeling of loss is too much to handle!"

Thomas hurried over to Sandy's apartment, attempting to stay within the speed limit. He thought to himself, *the last thing I need is to get a ticket, causing more of a delay in getting to the hospital.*

All Thomas could think about was Mr. Danforth. Surely, Maggie had already called him, and he would be at the hospital soon. *What do I say? How can I comfort him?*

Thomas thought about the time he'd known Mr. Danforth, realizing that he had been carrying this burden for some time. Trying to manage a huge corporation, and at the same time worrying about his grandson was a lot to handle. He was such a strong man. Thomas prayed that God would give him the right words to say. At the same time, he wondered, *why do we always think we have to say something. Maybe, sometimes, just being a friend and listening is enough.*

Sandy was waiting downstairs for Thomas and jumped into the car.

"I am so sorry, Sandy," Thomas said, attempting to comfort her. She couldn't say a word, and he could see that she was very distraught.

Thomas tried to imagine what she might be feeling. *This is the very first patient she has lost. But it's worse because Micah was more than a patient to her. God assigned him to her, and there's no doubt that she crossed that "imaginary" professional line emotionally. But, Dear Lord, how does a person keep from being emotionally attached when working with these children?*

After parking the car, Thomas and Sandy took the elevator to the fifth floor, past the nurses' station, to Micah's room. They had already moved Micah, and the white hospital bed was empty. Mr. Danforth was on the other side of the room looking out the window and resting his hand on Maggie's shoulder. She was seated next to him. Maggie looked up as they entered, putting her hand out for Sandy. Maggie and Sandy embraced, sharing tears that neither could stop.

Mr. Danforth didn't move. Thomas walked slowly to him. "I am so sorry, sir."

Turning around then, he looked directly at Thomas, "You were right, Thomas, in what you said earlier."

Thomas frowned, unsure what Mr. Danforth was talking about.

"Life is too short," Mr. Danforth said, answering Thomas's unasked question. "Thank you for bringing that chess set. You gave me quite a gift. I will forever see Micah and me playing that last game of chess. Thank you, Thomas."

"You are so welcome, sir, I am glad you had that time, too. We just want to let you know that Sandy and I are here for you and Maggie."

"Thank you," he said again, sadly.

Months of knowing this day would come did not take the sting away. It still hurt, and the empty bed where Micah once lay called out in deep sorrow. There was a terrible emptiness lingering in the air. Thomas had only met Micah once, but even for him the impact was huge.

Sandy and Thomas sat with Maggie and Mr. Danforth for the next hour, but it was soon time for everyone to leave. They gathered together Micah's belongings and walked to the car. After saying their sad goodbyes, Thomas and Sandy headed home. There was a sadness in the air that neither of them could shake. There was one less smile to look upon, one less beautiful presence in the world, and the hardest part of all would be learning to live without Micah.

Dear God, how does one forget a child like that, Sandy thought once she was home. She knelt beside her bed, praying for Maggie and Mr. Danforth. She prayed that they would be able to find peace and happiness in time. She knew in her heart that they would still be friends way past the many walls of the hospital.

It almost did not matter anymore about their move to China. Sandy felt peace with the thought either way. She had a sort of calm in knowing that life happens, and living life is out of our control most of the time. There was no need to become worried or tired, or to question or over-think it. It just did not matter the same way anymore. Sandy and Thomas had both decided to rest in whatever came their way, since even the best-laid plans can change in a moment. Closing her eyes, Sandy offered up one last prayer.

"Micah, please sleep well, sweetheart. Although you are absent from us here on earth, I know that you are present with our God and his angels in a much better place. Thank you for being the best boyfriend I have ever had! Just don't tell Thomas. We'll miss you."

Chapter Nine

❊

The Memorial and Funeral

Ted Danforth grieved deeply through the whole tragedy. He knew that Maggie was suffering and that they had to remain strong together. He was miserable in the painful feeling that parents are never supposed to outlive their children, much less their grandchildren.

While consoling Maggie, he said, "I have had to bury my wife, my son, and now my grandson. Where is the justice in all of this?"

No one ever wants to think about death, and they certainly don't expect tragedies to occur, such as losing a wife or son, but it is often good to be prepared for the worst. Ted Danforth knew that grief in itself was difficult to handle and that having things prepared, such as a pre-arranged plot, would alleviate at least some of the decisions and ease the burden on the family.

Maggie, on the other hand, often felt the opposite. In spite of numerous online guides for planning a memorial service and funeral, Maggie did not want a cookie-cutter service. She felt the need to plan everything herself, perhaps as part of her mourning. She had seen funerals that were a celebration of life, while others were solemn and depressing. Some families had even hired professional mourners! Through all of the ideas, Maggie's mind was overwhelmed with one decision after another—the obituary, open or closed casket, service handouts, guest book, choosing a minister, collecting pictures and stories, the selection of music, eulogies, and even what Micah would wear. More than anything, Maggie wanted Micah's message to be heard. It had to be personal. *What would Micah want to say if he were present? What is his message to everyone?*

It was quickly evident to Maggie that she needed help. She decided to call Sandy for support. Sandy accepted immediately. In spite of having no idea what she could actually do to help, she knew that Maggie needed her emotional support more than anything. That was the most important thing.

A memorial service was scheduled for Tuesday morning at the Cornerstone Christian Fellowship Church where Mr. Danforth had once attended. There would be an open gathering of family and friends, fellow church members, and the hospital staff that had been close to Micah. Several St. Louis Cardinals Baseball players asked Maggie if they could serve as pallbearers, including

Mitchell Thompson. She agreed, deeply appreciative of the fact that they cared so much for Micah.

Pastor Michael Sauder would open the memorial in prayer. Micah would certainly have wanted everyone in attendance to come to know Jesus Christ. Sandy thought this was a perfect opportunity to share their faith and the hope for eternity with non-believing family and friends.

Afterward, a funeral service for Micah would be held at Craighousers Funeral Home and Cemetery in Brentwood. Micah would be buried in a family plot that Mr. Danforth had purchased when his wife passed away. Tom was also buried there, and Maggie liked to think of them all being together.

Large double doors were opened in the front of the church as guests filed in. Each one signed the guest book before taking their seat, and some left short messages next to their names. Slowly, the church reached full capacity. Pictures of Micah's young life were displayed on large monitors. Light filtered into the room through beautiful stained glass windows that seemed to reach toward heaven itself. Maggie decided to play songs from Micah's iPod during the service.

Maggie, Mr. Danforth, Sandy, Thomas, and other close family members were seated in the first two rows. Micah's favorite song, "Feels Like I'm Born Again" by Third Day, was playing softly in the background at exactly ten o'clock as the memorial began. Maggie knew how much that song meant to Micah, but she had never earnestly listened to the words before. Now, as she listened, a gleam of bright light seemed to rest directly upon Micah's casket.

Maggie leaned over, tears in her eyes, and whispered in Ted's ear, "Micah is watching!"

Pastor Sauder approached the pulpit to welcome the guests to the memorial service. "Please bow your heads for a moment of prayer. 'Dear God, we thank You for the many things we have learned from Micah. Micah has taught me that age is just a number. His young life was an example that we are to follow. We are never guaranteed tomorrow, and living for today in faith is what matters most in life.'"

After concluding the prayer, several others were asked to come forward to say a few words. Everyone had beautiful things to say about the young boy.

Finally, Maggie walked to the pulpit to close the memorial service. Her body was trembling, and she had a hard time keeping herself calm. She whispered to herself as she slowly approached the pulpit, "Lord, give me the strength to deliver Micah's message of hope. Let me be strong for Micah's sake!"

The open casket was facing away from her, so she could not look directly at Micah's face. With her body shaking and tears still filling her eyes, it was obvious that she was distraught beyond imagination. Her heart was pounding within her chest, and it was all she could do to contain her emotions.

Maggie unfolded her notes, laying them carefully on the pulpit. She looked out across the congregation at those in attendance and seemed to be studying each face.

She recognized family and close friends, but there were many in attendance that she was not familiar with. After the memorial service she would learn that many in attendance were Micah's friends from Facebook who had come to pay their respects.

Clearing her throat, she nervously shared her first thoughts, "Honestly, I have been struggling to find the right words Micah would have me say to you. You see, Micah had an impact on everyone he spoke to or hung around with. He was an inspiration to other kids with cancer, doctors and nurses who were treating him, as well as those that could not believe his strong will to survive. His reach was far and wide. Rather than choosing my own words, I would like to use his."

Looking down at the paper, she read Micah's words, " 'Don't be sad for me because tonight I will be in Heaven.' Those were some of the last words Micah said before he passed, in a message he sent to those close to him."

She paused, taking a moment to breathe slowly and remain calm, "I believe Micah understood that happiness can be found in any situation if you look hard enough. Happiness isn't found in a single moment in time, but it's cherished by memories and developed through relationships we make from one moment to the next. Micah knew his life on earth would not last forever, but he held on to the hope of living forever with God. That was the true source of his strength. I would say that he chose faith and hope over the reality of his illness. He is indeed in Heaven right now, in the arms of God, and I will surely miss him."

Maggie slowly folded the note and stepped down from the pulpit. She had managed to say everything loud and clear but not without quite a few tears. While wiping her eyes, she took her seat next to her father-in-law.

Pastor Sauder thanked everyone for attending, calling on Mr. Craighouser, the funeral home director, to provide some general instructions for the funeral.

"Ladies and gentlemen," Mr. Craighouser said, standing near the pulpit, "Micah will be laid to rest in the Craighouser Cemetery in Brentwood. Please allow family members to exit first and lead the procession. Everyone else may follow in line. A police escort will be provided. Thank you."

Maggie, Ted, and other family members stayed seated for a few minutes to watch Micah's casket close. Maggie wept uncontrollably now, as only a mother can for her child. Mr. Danforth attempted to comfort her but knew nothing would ever truly work.

Sandy and Thomas consoled them as well, sharing tears together. After Micah's casket was lifted into the hearse and the door was closed, Sandy and Thomas pulled their car up behind the hearse, helping Maggie and Mr. Danforth inside. Slowly, the procession pulled away toward the cemetery.

Ted Danforth was all too familiar with the location. He had buried two loved ones there, and frequently visited their graves. A beautiful plot was already prepared for Micah, adorned with many wreaths and flowers. The casket was unloaded from the hearse by several St. Louis

Cardinal Baseball players, and he was laid to rest according to a traditional Christian burial, with the head of the casket on the western side. With a sob, Maggie knelt before the fresh tombstone, touching Micah's name tenderly, as she whispered his birth and death dates that had been scribed on the smooth, white marble. She couldn't watch them lower her baby into the ground. Behind her, her father-in-law stood near, his own tears flowing as he watched.

Pastor Sauder recited the 23rd Psalm as flowers were dropped onto the casket, and Micah was covered in his final resting place.

"The Lord is my shepherd; I shall not want. He maketh me to lie down in green pastures: he leadeth me beside the still waters ... "

As Pastor Sauder continued, the words slowly faded in Maggie's ears as an emptiness filled her, and she felt as if a part of her was being laid to rest with Micah.

Chapter Ten

※

The Decision Draws Nigh

few days had gone by since Micah's funeral. Sandy had returned to work and was now working with another child, this time a little girl with curly hair and a timid smile. Her name was Sarah. The news regarding Thomas's move to China was less of a distraction now that Sandy poured her life into her work at the hospital.

Thomas, on the other hand, simply accepted the idea that he would be going to China. He had decided it would be best to wait for Mr. Danforth to approach him under the circumstances. Micah's passing had occurred so soon after their talk and Mr. Danforth was so full of grief that Thomas wondered if he would even remember it.

That question was answered when he finally received a call to meet with Mr. Danforth at nine o'clock sharp on the upcoming Tuesday. For Thomas, there was an intense uneasiness about the whole situation. Would it be the news he and Sandy had been waiting for? They weren't harboring any expectations anymore, but that didn't keep their emotions from churning inside them.

Since Micah's death, Sandy and Thomas had both changed their thinking. They had decided to put all their faith in God and His plan, whatever that would be. Sometimes in life, things do not go the way we want, but when we realize the bigger picture, we achieve the greater good as God leads and we follow. There is often a tearing away and a building up within one's life that sets you on your path. They had reached this point in their life, and were letting God take control.

Tuesday morning came slowly, and Thomas felt the need to get on his knees and ask God for wisdom. He pondered on a verse that God brought to his thoughts. *"My thoughts are not your thoughts," says the LORD. "And my ways are far beyond anything you could ask or think."*

Thomas found some comfort in understanding these words and taking them to heart.

When he had calmed down, he made his way to Mr. Danforth's office and, for the third time, sat on the long, black leather couch. Thomas's foot did not do its usual tapping, and his countenance was calm and serious. He felt his heart and mind were conscious of the words that God had given him that morning. There were no late night rehearsals this time around, no prepared notes, and the point of worrying about the situation certainly had already passed. Thomas did not even consider having a counter offer in mind. He would accept God's plan, however it came to him.

"Mr. Mitchell," Alice said from her desk, "Mr. Danforth will see you now."

The secretary ushered him into the office, gave him an encouraging smile, and closed the door behind her.

Mr. Danforth was sitting behind his big desk, his face stern and unmoving.

"Good morning, Thomas," he said. "Please, come in and sit down."

"Hello, Mr. Danforth, it's a pleasure to see you again."

Thomas felt slightly uncomfortable now, not knowing how Mr. Danforth would respond to him in an office setting. After all, their relationship had somewhat changed to a more personal level.

After a quiet moment, Thomas casually asked, "How is Maggie doing?"

He thought it best not to mention Micah, as the wounds were too fresh.

"It has been a trying time," Mr. Danforth said, staring down at his hands and nodding slowly. "Thomas, would you be so kind as to join me at my game table?"

Thomas turned and looked across the room toward that small table against the wall where they had sat before. He noticed that the chess set he had bought Micah was all set up.

Thomas nodded. He was not the least bit surprised at this gesture and understood that the memory of Micah would never go away. Nor should it. Mr. Danforth stood up, and the two of them selected seats. Thomas sat across from Mr. Danforth with the chess set between them.

Mr. Danforth smiled and asked, "Would you like to play a friendly game of chess, if you have time?"

Thomas had a lot on his mind at that moment, and the idea of playing chess with Mr. Danforth threw him off a bit, but he nodded again.

"Black or white?" asked Mr. Danforth.

"Sorry?" Thomas asked, not understanding.

Mr. Danforth laughed, "Your pieces. White or black?"

Thomas grinned, "Well, white moves first, so I choose white."

Mr. Danforth held out a hand in a gesture that told Thomas he was supposed to begin. He stared at the board, thinking of his first move, and the game began.

"Thomas," Mr. Danforth asked while he was waiting, "would you say life is like a game of chess?"

Looking up, Thomas felt slightly nervous all over again, "Yes, sir, I guess you could say that."

Mr. Danforth continued as they played, moving pieces around the board one by one, "You see, Thomas, we all are pawns in this great big world, just trying to get to the other side, wouldn't you say?"

"Yes, sir, I can agree with that."

"Here's the thing … there are always roadblocks, bad directions, wrong turns, and such. You know, things that keep us from getting to other side. Don't you agree?"

"Yes, sir," Thomas said, keeping his eye on the board

as they played.

"Thomas, in my umpteen years with this company, I have concluded that we do the very best we can in life and move in different directions until we feel it's the right time and the safe thing to do. Very rarely do we intentionally sabotage our own plans. Agree?"

Feeling slightly philosophical, Thomas made another move and replied, "Well, sir, I would say we want to win in the game of life, but sometimes we can't control how things turn out."

"I understand your point, and agree, but let me ask you another question. What do we win when we get to the other side? What matters most? Is it winning, or is it how we've played the game?"

Thomas made a move and knew he had made a wise choice. "Check, sir!"

"Nice move there, Thomas!" exclaimed Mr. Danforth, examining the board for possibilities.

"Thank you, sir," Thomas said, smiling.

The temperament of Mr. Danforth suddenly went from calm to serious as he ignored the game for a moment and began to speak about his son.

"After my wife died, I lost my heart. But when Tom died too, I felt as if my right arm had been ripped off my body. Not only had I lost my son but also my partner, the one who would occupy this very office one day. I had such big dreams for my son. Not long after he died, I found a letter he had written to me in college that he never sent. In it, he told me that he wanted to be a doctor and had no passion for the career I'd chosen for him. Imagine that, a doctor. I remember being devastated! I'd wanted him to be an engineer like his ole man. I'd pushed and pushed until he gave up his dream of becoming a doctor and eventually gave in just to please me. In the end, it didn't matter. He was taken from me too soon. I no longer had my only son, and there was no one to take over the company I had built from the ground up."

He looked back at the board and moved a piece, taking a deep breath. Thomas was moved that Mr. Danforth was speaking to him so frankly, but he was still only half listening and continued to play the game as if his job depended on it. He made another move.

"Checkmate, sir!"

Not hearing him, Mr. Danforth continued talking, "Thomas, I have made many mistakes in my life, but … wait. Checkmate?"

"Yes, sir."

Mr. Danforth paused, looking at the board and realizing that he had just been moving the pieces without any serious thought or tactics. It wasn't very like him.

"Well, I see I need to practice more. Good job, Thomas. Anyway, I would like for you to work for me. With me, really. We would work side by side, if you are willing. You'd be staying here, obviously. Sandy could finish her residency. You can get married, have children of your own, and live the life you're looking for. What do you say?"

Thomas stared at Mr. Danforth without speaking. He was in shock, trying to take in what he had just heard.

Never in a million years did he consider anything like this. Not only would he not have to move, but he would be working with Mr. Danforth himself!

"Mr. Danforth, I would be honored to work with you, by your side!"

Mr. Danforth smiled, "By the way, out of curiosity, what did your dad want you to be?"

"My dad wanted me to take over the family winery in St. James."

Mr. Danforth replied with a playful grin, "I hope that was for distribution and not consumption!"

They both smiled, and Mr. Danforth continued, "Oh, Thomas, as fathers we think we are doing the best we can at the time. Thankfully, you seem to have stood up to your father and did what you felt was the right thing for you. If only things had been different for Tom and me."

Mr. Danforth looked at him seriously, "I do not want you to think I am trying to replace my son, as if that were even possible. But I am asking you to fill a sort of void in my heart where he once was. I need someone who can respect others and have the decency to look beyond their own needs. I respect you as a person, Thomas, and as an asset to this company. Besides, Sandy has many more children, mothers, and fathers that will need her help. Not to mention that Maggie would be lost without Sandy's friendship, and for that I am also grateful."

Thomas wanted to jump up and down and shout for joy, but his emotions would have to wait. He kept a serious face as he took in this fantastic news.

Mr. Danforth reached over and put his hand on Thomas's shoulder. "Now, having said all that, there may come a time when I will need you to go to China to represent this company, but only after Sandy finishes her training. Does that sound like a plan you both can live with?"

"Yes, sir," Thomas said, his voice trembling with excitement. "I don't know what to say! But, thank you! Thank you so much! I will not let you down."

Mr. Danforth began to place the pieces back in their places on the chessboard. He looked at Thomas, "I think a rematch is in order, don't you?"

"Yes, sir, indeed I do!" Thomas said laughing, and a new game began.

Thomas could not wait to tell Sandy the good news. After another game of chess, he sprinted out of the office with an uncontrollable happiness. Not only had God answered their prayers in a miraculous way, but He also seemed to be carefully putting pieces of a greater puzzle together. Thomas didn't know it, but this was God's ultimate playbook.

Thomas thought about how all of their lives had been intertwined by the hand of God. They were truly blessed to see the fruition of much prayer and to see how God could make something grow out of sorrow and loss. Only a loving God could restore and mend broken hearts in this way.

Thomas hurried to the hospital, hoping to find Sandy. He did not bother to call her first. He was simply too excited. He made his way to the nurse's desk and politely asked them to page her. It was not long before she was walking down the hall toward him. Looking up, she was automatically concerned. Thomas had never come to her work and paged her before.

"Hi, Thomas. Are you okay?" Sandy asked with a frown.

Thomas was nearly bursting with excitement. "Oh, baby, everything is great! Mr. Danforth has offered me a position to work beside him! We do not have to go to China, and you can finish your residency!"

Sandy was stunned for only a moment, and then she almost jumped into Thomas's arms, forgetting she was at work. She was overcome with joy at the surprising news.

Mustering some composure, she gripped Thomas's hands, "Oh, honey, this is unbelievable! I simply cannot believe it!"

She paused, and then her smile grew, "Oh, wait, yes, I can. We serve an awesome God, don't we?"

Thomas looked at Sandy and suddenly felt as if his very soul was overflowing with love and happiness. Taking a deep breath, with everyone watching, he bent down onto one knee. In front of patients, nurses, and doctors, he asked, "Sandy, will you make me the most blessed man on earth and marry me?"

The entire room seemed to freeze, waiting to see what would happen. A few of Sandy's co-workers called out shouts of encouragement. Sandy turned so many shades of red she looked like she might be sick, but Thomas could tell she was just very happy.

"Oh, yes, Thomas! Yes, I will marry you!"

Everyone started clapping and cheering them on.

Thomas got up from his knee and hugged her, wanting to raise her up in his arms and spin her around. Unable to contain a smile that stretched from ear to ear, he reassured Sandy, "Tonight, we will celebrate, set the date, call our folks, and anything else we can think of. I have to get back to work, but I wanted to deliver the news in person. And then I couldn't help myself! I love you, Sandy, and thank you for making me the happiest man on earth."

Sandy knew she had to hurry back to work, so she offered a quick kiss, "I love you, too!"

They embraced again, squeezing one another as if they would never see each other again. They both thought they would simply melt from how happy they were. Then, trying to stay focused, they said their goodbyes and separated, still smiling.

Sandy returned to her duties with a joy in her heart beyond any she had felt before and a beautiful smile that made the rooms light up. She thought to herself, I just got a two-for-one blessing! I am getting married to the man of my dreams, and we are not leaving for China!

On the way to the car, Thomas thought about the most beautiful woman he had ever met and how she would soon be his wife.

Chapter Eleven

✳

Wherever He Leads, I'll Go

*T*homas and Sandy continued to grow in both their careers and their relationship. They had found a small, intimate church in the area and were sure they had found the place that God was calling them to serve. Pastor John was a wonderful young and energetic pastor with a heartfelt passion for young people and the missions of God.

Six months had passed since Thomas proposed, and Thomas and Sandy were finally sitting down to talk about their plans over a quiet dinner. The night of the proposal, they had decided on a June wedding, as the lease on Thomas's apartment would end then.

They had called their family to share the wonderful new decision. The family was thrilled at the engagement and gave them their blessings. Now the date was inching closer, and the preparations were becoming more of a reality.

They had known for years that they were going to get married, but it seemed surreal now that the date was set and it was finally going to happen. Sitting at the dining table, Sandy was suddenly overwhelmed by emotion and began to cry. Thomas was taken aback, worried that something was wrong.

"Sandy, are you okay, honey? What's wrong?"

Looking at Thomas with tears streaming down her face, she said, "I am just so happy, Thomas. All my dreams are coming true."

Over the course of those months, they had learned a lot through the process of planning and working together. Sandy realized that she needed to trust Thomas more in the decisionmaking processes, and Thomas discovered that he needed to be a better listener, instead of just trying to have answers for everything. Sandy found it ironic that, in their careers, these traits were beneficial to them, but in their personal lives, they would have to shift gears to work with each other.

Pastor John would perform their wedding, and there was no question about who would be giving away the bride. Sandy, like many girls, had always dreamed of her father walking her down the aisle on her wedding day. They were very close.

During the months of planning, they often talked on the phone about the big day. He would tease her that he was going to super glue their hands together so that he would not have to give her away when they arrived at the altar. The calls never lasted long, however. Her dad would get choked up when he thought about his little girl getting married and would have to hang up. Sandy could hear him struggling just to say, "Sandy, I've got to go. Love ya, honey!"

She would then hear the click and the dial tone. She knew he respected Thomas. He always called him his son, rather than his future son-in-law, but it was hard for him to let his little girl go.

Sandy's dad could always make her laugh. It would take a really big man to gain the same respect Sandy had for her dad. Thomas was just that man. When a girl has a strong father figure, her expectations for the man in her life are set higher.

Sandy had never considered that her dad might not be around forever. God's playbook was opened once again, putting another plan into action, and soon a tragic phone call would push her faith and leave Sandy questioning her God.

"Hello?" Sandy spoke as she picked up the phone.

"Sandy, honey, its mom! Come home, baby. Daddy is really sick! You have to come home."

Sandy could hear a tremor in her mother's voice and didn't ask any questions, "I will book a flight and be there as soon as I can."

Sandy knew her dad had not been feeling well. He always blamed it on bouts of indigestion, and no one could get him to go to the doctor.

Hanging up the phone, Sandy had no idea that her

mother was withholding the truth from her that her father was already gone. For Sandy's sake, her mom thought it was best for Sandy to get home before learning the truth. She prayed that Thomas would come with her, knowing that Sandy would need him. Nothing would have prepared Sandy to face her father's death.

Sandy made a quick call to Thomas as she packed a small bag. Thomas spoke with Mr. Danforth who insisted on flying Thomas and Sandy in his small jet.

Pulling up to her parent's house, Sandy felt like some-one had kicked her in the gut. She had a strong feeling of dread, and something told her that her dad was worse than she had been told.

Dashing in the house, the first thing she saw was her mother sitting in her dad's favorite chair. Her mom stood, wrapping her arms around Sandy with a moan and sob-bing, "I am so sorry, honey! Daddy is gone. I couldn't tell you on the phone. I'm so sorry!"

Feeling suddenly numb in her mother's arms, Sandy froze, her body resisting all movement. Her mind seemed to go blank as the shock took over. She could not believe what she was hearing, "Mom, what happened?"

Her mother pulled away and placed her hands on Sandy's face, "He had a massive heart attack, and there was nothing they could do. It was all so sudden!"

Looking at her mom, Sandy didn't know what to say. There was a shocked, painful silence in the room as her mother gripped her again, sobbing onto her shoulder.

"I can't imagine my life without my dad," Sandy said,

finally. "He was everything to me."

"I'm so sorry, honey," Thomas said from behind them. "I'm really sorry."

"Mom, where is he? When is the funeral?" Sandy asked, trying to put aside the pain before she fell apart.

"The funeral is tomorrow, honey. I know it's soon. It's just, well, I wanted … I just thought it would be best."

Thomas reached over and wrapped his arms around both of them, holding Sandy and her mom tightly. They could all feel the void that her father had left. It appeared as if nothing would ever be the same. Sandy knew that she, at the very least, would never be the same.

The next day, Sandy walked into the church with Thomas on one side and her mother on the other. Seeing the casket, she thought to herself, *my dad is not there. My dad is not in there. It is an empty shell.*

On this day, Sandy was thankful for her beliefs. She held Thomas's hand so tightly that her fingers cramped. Though no words were exchanged between them, a quiet resignation settled over the couple.

The words the pastor spoke during the service washed over them like a healing balm. In the end, it was the song that played as she said her last goodbye that touched Sandy the most.

Placing a yellow rose across the casket, Sandy leaned close and whispered, "Bye, Daddy. I love you. I will see you again *up there*." She lifted her eye toward heaven.

Echoing softly through the church, the song continued to play.

"I come to the garden alone,
While the dew is still on the roses,
And the voice I hear falling on my ear
The Son of God discloses.

"And He walks with me, and he talks with me,
And He tells me I am his own;
And the joy we share as we tarry there,
None other has ever known."

Chapter Twelve

✳

The Wedding

fter Mr. Fogel's death, Thomas and Sandy kept saying that they would postpone the date for the wedding. After such a loss it felt like too much to bear. But as June drew near, they eventually decided it was time.

Sandy tried to avoid thinking about her father being gone. The stress of considering who might walk her down the aisle was more than she could bear. She missed her father, and the thought of him not being at her wedding broke her heart.

Suddenly it struck her who she could ask to stand in for her father. When she told Thomas, he smiled ear to ear and gave her a big hug. She would ask Mr. Danforth to walk her down the aisle. After all, he and Maggie had become such a huge part of their lives that it seemed he would be the perfect one.

Ted and Thomas had spent many hours working together, and Maggie still volunteered at the hospital as often as she could. Working with other sick children, she had become a strong support for many families since Micah's death. Sandy was very proud just to know her.

Sandy set up an appointment with Mr. Danforth's office since she knew he was a busy man. She also made sure that Thomas could attend.

On the day of the meeting, Sandy walked into Mr. Danforth's office, greeting his secretary for the first time. Alice smiled and ushered Sandy back toward the office right away. Ted was glad to see her and immediately pulled her into a big hug with an even bigger smile.

"To what do I owe this wonderful visit?" Ted asked.

Looking at Mr. Danforth, Sandy smiled and started speaking, still a little nervous, "I have something important to ask you, but I would like to wait for Thomas, if you don't mind."

Just then, Thomas came through the door. He greeted Sandy with a quick kiss on the cheek and shook hands with Mr. Danforth.

"So, have I missed anything?" Thomas asked.

"No, I just got here," Sandy said with a smile. "We were waiting for you."

Mr. Danforth asked Thomas and Sandy to sit down on the curved seats to which Thomas had become so accustomed, and the couple exchanged a glance.

She had thought about her words very carefully, but suddenly, tears welled up in her eyes. She looked at Mr.

Danforth and took a deep breath, "Ted, you know my father passed away a few months ago. Along with his death, my hopes and dreams of him walking me down the aisle were shattered. But …" she paused, taking another deep breath, "after much prayer, I felt in my heart that I should ask you to take his place for this special moment. I cannot think of anyone who is more close to our hearts than you. Mr. Danworth, would you do me the honor of walking me down the aisle for our wedding?"

Mr. Danforth was clearly emotionally shaken, and for a moment he stared wide-eyed at the young couple, until he sat down so quickly that his chair rocked backwards. After a moment, he looked up at Thomas and Sandy and whispered, "I feel so honored that you would ask me, Sandy."

"Does that mean yes, sir?" Sandy asked, her voice and body trembling in anticipation.

With a speed that surprised them, Ted jumped from his seat and came around the desk, wrapping his long arms around both of them.

"Yes, yes, and yes!" he said, practically shouting. "So when is this special day supposed to take place?"

Thomas piped up enthusiastically, "We have decided on June 15th, sir. Will that work for you?"

Ted pulled out his calendar and began scanning his appointments, "I would say June 15th is perfect, but I have only one more thing to add."

They both looked at Mr. Danforth with a small amount of concern until he looked back up at them with a face-splitting grin, "I would like to take care of all expenses for the wedding. And the honeymoon! No arguments! End of discussion!"

Thomas and Sandy looked at each other in disbelief. They were speechless as they turned to look at Mr. Danforth with mouths wide open.

"Oh, sir … thank you! Thank you so very much! We don't know what to say," Thomas said, standing again and shaking his hand all over again.

Sandy offered a tearful thank you as well, unable to contain her emotions. She stood up, and they both offered Mr. Danforth a warm hug.

"You don't have to say a word," Mr. Danforth replied. "Family is everything to me, and this is just a small token from a blessed man. You've been so good to Maggie and me, you're practically family now. It makes me very happy to do this for you both."

Thomas and Sandy could not wait to tell their families the good news. They said their goodbyes to Mr. Danforth, still grinning and laughing, and sprinted out of his office.

Later that evening, Thomas and Sandy began to make the endless phone calls to family and friends. Their families reacted with surprise and great excitement. Hanging up the phone after reaching the last person on their list, Thomas let out a much-needed sigh of relief. Looking at Sandy, he could see that she had drifted into a state of deep thinking. Her eyebrows were crinkled and she was staring out into nothingness.

"Now for the hard part," she said to Thomas.

"What do you mean, honey? What hard part?" he asked, unsure.

Sandy smiled a little, taking a deep breath, "I have to find the perfect dress, the flowers, the cake, the invitations …" She threw her hands up into the air with an exaggerated groan, her smile wider, "Uggghh … so many details!"

Thomas gazed at her with a loving smile on his face, "I cannot wait for you to become my wife, Sandy."

Time seemed to passed quickly, and the wedding day arrived faster than anyone could have expected. With the help of Maggie and Sandy's mom, Sandy and Thomas had spent the last few weeks making all of the arrangements. They had decided it would be a very small wedding, with only immediate family and a few friends. Sandy and her mom found the perfect dress at one of the vintage wedding Boutiques in St. Louis, and they had worked out all of the extra details as a group.

Sandy tried not to think too much about her father and his absence. Instead, she felt as if he would be looking down on her on her special day. She even placed a small picture of him inside her bouquet as her way of having him with her when she walked down the aisle. Sandy stood in the dressing room looking at herself in the mirror.

The dress had a style to it that was almost kimono-like. It was made of soft, white silk, with a v-line neckline and cap sleeves. It was a perfect fit to her small frame and reached almost to her ankles. Small, delicate flowers embroidered in the silk decorated the dress in tiny, graceful patterns that could barely be seen except up close. Sandy's hair was pulled back into a perfect French twist, and her mother had given her small pearl earrings that added just enough jewelry to the beautiful ensemble. Over her hair, she wore a white hat that featured a satin flower, feather, and bead ornament. It had a simple attached lace veil that draped just over her nose, concealing her eyes. Finally, elegant silver high-heeled shoes with crystal accents adorned her feet, perfecting the graceful look.

She carried a bouquet of white roses with a single light purple Asian Orchid lying neatly in the center. As she looked herself over, she began to wonder how Thomas was doing and if he was nervous.

Across the church, Thomas was, indeed, a little nervous. He stood looking into his father's eyes as his dad attempted to straighten Thomas's tie one more time. Thomas was wearing a three button, single-breasted jacket with a notch lapel. The lapel was triple-pleated satin with a self-top collar. He wore a light lavender shirt underneath. A small orchid, matching the one in Sandy's bouquet, was pinned delicately to his lapel. Thomas was thinking about his wedding night. They had waited for so long, and he knew God had blessed this marriage, but he was starting to get a little emotional.

"Son, are you okay?" his father asked, concerned.

He could tell by the stern, distant look on Thomas's face that something was weighing heavily on his heart.

"Yes, sir, I'm so happy!" Thomas said without hesitating, then paused. "I mean, well, Dad, you know

Sandy and I ... well, we have never been together. We've been waiting for this time. I'm not sure how ... well, I'm not sure how it's going to go."

His dad placed one hand on his shoulder, and said, with confidence, "Thomas, God knew all about these things way before the instruction manuals were ever written. Everything will be all right. The natural course of things will just kick in. Making love is a beautiful thing. Your marriage bed will be a sacred place. I am so proud of you, son, for being strong and for standing up for what you believe all this time."

Thomas looked at his father with a shy smile, "It was not easy, Dad, believe me. But it seemed like when I was weak, she was strong, and when she was weak, I was strong. God helped us to get to this day."

Suddenly, there was a knock at the door, and Mr. Danforth poked his head in, telling them it was time.

"So, any last thoughts, Thomas?" he asked, smiling.

"Yes. Tell Sandy I love her."

Thomas followed his father out the door and down the long corridor to the chapel. They made their way through the side door, entering the chapel from the side. Thomas looked around to see a small congregation of friends and family. He nodded his head to a few smiling faces, smiling back. He then took his place near Pastor John.

Thomas had not seen the inside of the chapel since their mothers had decided they would be the ones to decorate it. Besides Sandy picking out a candlelight service and a color scheme, everything else had been left to them. Sandy gave up this task gladly, knowing they had great taste and trusting them completely.

Thomas surveyed the church with a quick glance, recognizing the beautiful purple orchids and jasmine flowers covering the archway. Each bench was decorated with white lace at the end of the pew with two to three orchids in the center. The scenery was simple, but elegant in every way. Candles were lit along the walls, emitting a strong jasmine fragrance while casting a dim but beautiful, flickering light over the room. He saw Maggie, the matron of honor, already standing across the aisle with her delicate bouquet of orchids and jasmine and wearing a simple, elegant lavender dress. Thomas gave her a nervous but excited smile.

The pastor nodded to the organist, and the wedding song began. The double doors opened slowly, revealing Sandy and Mr. Danforth. Thomas's heart began to race, and he forgot to breathe for a moment. She was lovely. Sandy put her arm in the crook of Ted's arm, and he placed his hand over hers gently.

Looking at Sandy he whispered, "It is my honor to walk you down the aisle, Sandy. You look very beautiful."

Sandy smiled as she fought back a nervous tear, and they began their slow march down the aisle. She glanced around at the beauty of the room and looked up to see Thomas standing tall and handsome at the altar, smiling at her. Her heart beat faster, and she could feel her palms sweating as she held tightly to the bouquet. Reaching the archway, they paused as Pastor John asked who would give this bride.

Sandy's mom joined Mr. Danforth, and they said in unison, "Her father and I do."

Sandy hugged her mom, then Mr. Danforth. With tears in her eyes, she took Thomas's hand.

Thomas and Sandy had written their own vows and now felt blessed that they could say them to each other. Thomas looked into Sandy's eyes through her delicate veil, his heart filled with so much love he felt like he was basking in it. With a smile filled with that love, he began to say his heartfelt words, "Sandy, thank you for loving me. Thank you for standing beside me all these years. I promise I will love you like our Father in Heaven loves us, unconditionally and forever, taking care of you, honoring you, and respecting you as my wife."

Sandy looked into his eyes and prayed she could say the words as eloquently as he just had.

Taking a deep breath and drawing strength from the love she saw in his eyes, she began, "I will cherish our union and love you more each day than I did the day before. I will trust you and respect you, laugh with you and cry with you. I will love you faithfully, through good times and bad, regardless of the obstacles we may face. We will always overcome them together. I give you my hand, my heart, and my love."

Exchanging rings, the pastor pronounced them man and wife and finished with the wonderful ending, "You may kiss the bride."

Thomas lifted the small veil over her beautiful blue

eyes and gazed at her, unable to believe how blessed he was and how happy he was in this moment. After kissing her tenderly, they both said a small prayer, thanking God for this union.

Thomas and Sandy had the most wonderful honeymoon. It may not have been the most typical honeymoon, but it was special to them. They spent the week moving into a charming little farmhouse they had bought. Giving up both of their apartments, they were able to purchase this new home together.

The house sat on twenty acres surrounded by maple and walnut trees and overlooked the Mississippi River. It had a comfortable, classic feel to it, with a wood-burning stove and original wood floors. Walking out onto the wide wraparound porch, you could see a dock that went down to the river's edge. This home was truly a piece of heaven to Thomas and Sandy. It had belonged to Mr. and Mrs. Frederic Baker, who had recently decided to retire to Florida. They had raised all their children in this home and lived through many remarkable things.

It truly was a dream home, and one in which Thomas and Sandy could one day raise their own children. They had begun looking for a home months before the wedding, but had their eye on this one from the start. They knew it was important to have a place where they could get away from their busy, hectic jobs and feel truly at home.

Sandy was sure that Thomas's job would be secure enough, and with her having less than a year left of her residency, they were comfortable in their selection. The commute was slightly longer than what they had wanted, but they used that time to reflect and pray before their day began to unfold.

Upon selling the home, Mr. and Mrs. Baker had one request, and it was a rather large one. Every summer, they had hosted a weeklong retreat for children with disabilities and children with cancer in remission. Thomas and Sandy were amazed by this news and felt it was a God-given gift. They told the owners they would be proud to carry on the tradition.

The Bakers had been more than thrilled to find out that Thomas and Sandy were devoted Christians, and they were convinced God had provided a provision for these children while they were away. They had wanted to move a few years before but were not able to let go of this special program. Their church had started the program ten years earlier, and they had offered to let the church use their land. The church had built a bunkhouse for the children, and it had been a summer tradition ever since. So they kept praying for buyers who would carry the same heart for children as they had and felt blessed when Sandy and Thomas came around.

Thomas and Sandy were amazed at how the hand of God had moved them, placing them strategically where he would have them be. After a week of moving, they were able to visit the church that Mr. and Mrs. Baker had attended. It was a small church, and everyone was like family. Thomas and Sandy met with the pastor, who was thrilled that they had bought the Baker's home. He was even more thrilled that they would be carrying on the church's program.

Along with the Baker's initial request, there were a couple more strings attached to the house. In fact, Thomas and Sandy were now the proud owners of two pigs, a cow, three goats, a few chickens, and two horses named Mabel and Ernie. There was also an old farm hand named Gus living in a cabin on the edge of the property.

Gus had been with the Bakers the last ten years. He had been a drifter, homeless and without family, but Mrs. Baker said they had always had a soft spot in their hearts for the homeless and offered Gus a place to stay. He had said he would stay only if he could work for his keep, and he had tended to the animals and farmland ever since.

Mr. and Mrs. Baker had also invited Gus to join them for Sunday services many times, but Gus just smiled, declining every time. Mrs. Baker said Gus was a man of few words, feeling the pain he had endured in his lifetime was heavy on his heart. She knew that one day, though, God would bring him around in some way.

Mr. Baker had interrupted Mrs. Baker at that, sharing, "Maybe God will do a great work in him, or maybe he is fulfilling his destiny just as he is."

Mrs. Baker had smiled, giving him a kiss on the cheek, "I am sure you are right, dear."

When Thomas heard all this, he had squeezed Sandy's

hand tightly. They both knew God had just made another move in their lives. Mr. and Mrs. Baker had nothing but good things to say about Gus, and with their busy schedules, Sandy and Thomas were certain it would be nice to have his help on the farm.

Now, as she unpacked boxes and gazed out at the beautiful scenery around her new home, Sandy could still remember Mrs. Baker's words, "Who am I to say what God is doing in anyone's life. He has a plan and a calling for everyone, I know. We all are like pieces on a chess board."

To their surprise, Thomas and Sandy's first retreat would be in the first week of August, barely a few months away. There was much to do to get ready for the children who would be visiting their new farm, and they were eager to get started on the preparations.

Chapter Thirteen

✳

The Retreat

The end of July came much too quickly, and between their jobs and their new responsibilities on their farm, Sandy was feeling overwhelmed with everything they still needed to do.

"Thomas, did you get Gus to pick up the food yesterday?" Sandy called from the storage room, feeling very distracted. "What about the life vests? I'm afraid those old ones aren't going to work. We only have a week until the retreat!"

Thomas had gone outside to help Gus with the new chicken coop and did not hear Sandy calling to him. Coming back in a few minutes later, he found Sandy in the back of the house pulling blankets out of a couple of old trunks.

"Honey, I picked up the food this morning. The life vests, too," he said, dusting his hands off on his jeans,

"You can mark them off the list."

"Oh good," Sandy said, standing slowly and taking a deep breath. "You know, this is a lot of work. I really had no idea. It's lucky that I'm on break for a while and that Mr. Danforth gave you a couple weeks off."

Thomas shook his head, "Don't worry so much. Ted said he and Maggie are coming out to help this week. You know, I still stand amazed at how God has done such wonderful things in our lives."

Sandy put down the blankets and moved closer to Thomas. Putting her arms around his neck, she asked, "Have I told you today how much I love you?"

Thomas looked down at her sweet face with a smile to match hers, "Yes, but you can tell me again."

"I love you, Thomas," she said, her voice soft as she laid her head against his chest. They embraced each other, enjoying a few minutes of serene quiet. Thomas took a deep breath as he held her tight, thinking about how blessed he was. After a few moments, a loud rumbling noise from outside made them both jump in surprise.

"What in the world?" asked Thomas, heading out the door with Sandy close behind.

A huge semi-trailer truck had pulled up in front of the house, casting a wide shadow over the yard. Gus was beside the truck talking with a tall, gruff-looking man who handed him a piece of paper as he stepped down from the cab door.

"Good morning," Thomas said as he and Sandy approached the pair, "Can we help you?"

Gus spoke up first, "Thomas, looks like somebody named Ted Danforth sent you some things for the retreat. Do you know this fella?"

Thomas looked back at Sandy with a big smile, "We sure do."

Gus handed him the paper, and he looked it over. It was a list of the supplies that Ted had sent. As Thomas read it aloud, he and Sandy began to laugh. It started as a giggle and quickly grew into hysterical laughter until Thomas's phone began to ring.

Attempting to gain some composure, Thomas answered. "Yes, sir, it sure did!" he said after a pause. "Thank you, sir! I will, sir!"

Thomas hung up the phone. He glanced back at Sandy, and they both said in perfect unison, "Mr. Danforth!"

The old truck driver didn't seem to be in a mood for laughter and interrupted, "Don't mean to be a party pooper, but I gotta get this stuff unloaded. Where do you want it?"

Thomas looked at Sandy and then at Gus, a little bit lost. He pressed his lips together and raised his eyebrows, hoping Gus would offer his advice.

"Gus, what do you think?" he asked after a moment of silence. Gus surveyed the ground and thought about it before answering.

"There's a flat area over there," he said, pointing, "that would make a great place for the playground, and the aluminum boats can go down there by the docks. They're light enough to carry."

"The freezers can go in the outdoor kitchen by the bunkhouse," he continued after a short pause, gesturing toward the small building. "We had better get them hooked up fast, so all of those boxes of meat can be put up quick."

He looked back at the truck with a little frown, "That there bouncy thing, though ... well, I'll have to think on that for a bit."

"Thanks Gus ... I knew you would know," Thomas said with a relieved grin.

Once more, Thomas's phone rang. He answered it quickly, "Yes, sir. Oh, that's wonderful, sir. Thank you again, sir!"

Thomas clicked off the phone and turned to Sandy, "Mr. Danforth is sending over some men to help with putting up the playground and anything else we might need."

Before he had even gotten the words out of his mouth, a shiny, oversized pickup truck pulled up behind the semi. Four men waved at Thomas from the back, looking ready to work.

Thomas and Sandy smiled at such a blessing and waved back at the group. Gus walked away with a sigh. Scratching his head, he mumbled to himself, "I ain't never seen nothing like this in my whole life."

Monday morning came fast and furious, and as Thomas and Sandy watched, a herd of excited visitors exited the church bus. One by one, they counted five children and four adults. It was a much smaller group than they had expected, but that was just fine for their first go-around.

The adults were Peggy, a retired nurse; Mr. Perry, a retired school counselor; and Kelly and Mike, a married couple from the church, who all were willing to stay through the week. Ted and Maggie came early, ready to help. They went straight to the kitchen, cooking up a huge breakfast of bacon, eggs, and hash browns.

Since Sandy and Thomas were brand new to this kind of adventure, they were thankful for all the help they had. The volunteers had collaborated with Mr. and Mrs. Baker in organizing the retreat for many years and were dedicated and enthusiastic. They knew the art of advocating and encouraging these children to have a great time while taking their minds off their troubles.

Mike poked his head out of the bus door, "Hey, Thomas, can you give me a hand with the bags and this wheelchair?"

Thomas stepped up gladly and assisted Mike with unloading the bags and the wheelchair.

Suddenly, they heard a young voice calling, "Hey, what about me?"

Mike laughed as he hopped back up on the bus and lifted a young man into his arms. Carrying him down the bus steps, he placed him gently into the wheelchair.

"Thomas and Sandy, meet Sam. Sam, meet Thomas and Sandy!"

Sam looked up, smiling, "I know you … we met at

church! You're the ones that took over for Mr. and Mrs. Baker, right?"

Sandy spoke up, "That's exactly right, Sam! And we're looking forward to a great week. How about you?"

Sam looked at Mike and then back at them, "Do I smell bacon?" he asked, sniffing the air.

Without waiting for an answer, he began to wheel himself down the path toward the café. Sandy and Thomas looked at each other, grinning.

Mike handed them a list of all the children's names, emergency information, and releases from the parents. They noticed small notations beside each of their names, alerting them to their special needs.

"Kelly and I will get the children's bags to the bunkhouse!" said Mike with an enthusiastic smile. "If it's okay with you guys, we can then meet you in the café for some of that food."

Nearby, Mr. Perry and Peggy were busily arranging the children in some sort of order, so introductions could be made. Thomas and Sandy joined them, waving to all of the kids.

"Hello, Thomas. Hello, Sandy," the older man said. "I am Mr. Perry. Sorry I couldn't make the meeting last week. I think you'll remember Peggy, though."

"Nice to meet you both," said Thomas before turning toward the children who were standing quietly, waiting for the next move.

Thomas and Sandy offered them a big, "Good morning," before looking at the list. Thomas began to call each child by name, silently reading the notations that were written beside each name.

"Is there a Melanie here?" asked Thomas. *Mildly Autistic. May need redirection sometimes. She is verbal and able to express her wants and needs.*

A little girl with curly red hair and freckles slowly lifted her hand. She was wearing jeans and a green shirt that said Jesus Loves Me in bright pink letters.

"That's me, sir," Melanie said with a smile.

"Are you ready to have fun?" asked Sandy, bending down toward the girl.

"Yes, ma'am, I am!" replied Melanie, beaming.

Sandy then looked at the next name, "Do we have a Daniel?" *Leukemia. Has been in remission for the last two years. He is rather shy and withdrawn.*

Daniel raised his hand quickly and put it back down. Sandy noticed he was a rather small boy for his age. His file said that he was ten, but he looked as if he was six or seven. He had big blue eyes and soft blond hair, and instantly reminded Sandy of her little brother.

"I'm so happy you are here with us for the week," Sandy said, softly.

Daniel smiled and looked away.

Thomas read the next name out loud. "How about Sam?" *Wheelchair bound due to car accident at age five. He is now 12. Sam is very active and independent.*

With a smile, he remembered the boy in the wheelchair. He looked down at the children with a grin, "Oh, well ... you know, he appears to have been a bit hungry, and he already made his way to the café!"

He then read the next name, "So, do we have a Bethany here?"

No hands went up, but Thomas could see Peggy doing a sly gesture with her finger, pointing down at a girl with short brown hair and big, dark brown eyes.

Thomas raised his eyebrows and continued, "I am sure we have a Bethany on this list. I wonder where she has gone."

Suddenly a noticeable grin poured across the beautiful young face. Sandy stepped forward, kneeling down in front of the girl and said, "Could this be Bethany, the pretty girl with the pretty name?"

Bethany blinked up into Sandy's eyes, and whispered, "That's me."

Sandy whispered back, "Nice to meet you, Bethany."

Sandy stepped back and read Bethany's notations. *Has been in foster care the last two years. Has a very abusive background. She is seven and may need reassurance when in uncomfortable situations.*

Thomas read one last name, "Do we have a Larry here?" *Larry is in remission, as he suffered from a rare form of brain cancer. While the lesions were removed, it left him with a speech impediment. Sometimes Larry gets his words backwards, or forgets what he wants to say. This is very frustrating for him.*

A tall, thin boy raised his hand. "I … I'm Larry!"

Thomas stretched out his hand and shook Larry's hand, "Nice to meet you, Larry!"

Looking at the children, Thomas gave an enthusiastic shout, making even Sandy jump, "ARE YOU READY FOR BREAKFAST?"

In response, the children started jumping up and down, shouting, "YEAAAAAA!"

Like little ducks, the children fell in line, following Thomas and Sandy down the path to the café. The café was a small cabin that sat next to the bunkhouse. Five large wooden tables and benches took up the majority of the main room, with a little stage area at one end for any guest speakers.

The smell of bacon filled the air, and soon everyone was sitting together at the tables eating a wonderful breakfast. It did not take the children long to open up and to begin to talk to one another.

Thomas and Sandy sat back and watched the way the children interacted with one another. Larry had taken shy Bethany under his wing and was helping her open her drink.

"Beth," he started, then paused and cleared his throat. "May I call you Beth? Let me hold … I mean help … help you with your juice."

Bethany looked up at Larry and smiled, handing him her juice box.

It had been decided that Mike and Kelly would head all the activities. Thomas and Sandy were perfectly willing to help in any way they could, while still letting them be in charge.

When everyone seemed to be finishing up their food,

Mike stood on the stage area, raised above the tables, and clapped his hands to get the children's attention.

"HELLLOOO ... YOUNG GALS AND GUYS!" he shouted. "ARE YOU READY TO HAVE SOME FUN?"

With nervous smiles, the children gave a small "Yeah!"

It was not the level of cheer that Mike was waiting for, so he yelled again, "HELLLOOO ... YOUNG GALS AND GUYS! ARE YOU READY TO HAVE SOME FUN?"

This time the children clapped their hands and burst into a much louder, "YEAH!"

The schedule for the week was planned out so that the children would be enjoying a very busy week. Due to the heat in the afternoon, most of the outside activities would be done in the morning, with the warmer parts of the day left for doing arts and crafts. In the evening, there would be a special program to enjoy each night. Thursday was the last day, so that night would be filled with a special talent show in which the children would entertain their parents and staff, awards would be given out, and they could say their goodbyes.

After breakfast, the children gathered around Mike and Kelly for their first nature hike. Each child was given a backpack filled with water and snacks. The path was handicap accessible, perfect for the children to enjoy safely. Sam had attended the camp for several years in a row, and now knew this path very well, so he volunteered to be the leader.

After instructions, the group set off. Larry took Bethany's hand as Sam led the way. Melanie had to be reminded to stay on the path a few times. After a while, Thomas picked her up and placed her on his shoulders. She squealed with delight as she gazed around from her new height.

Thomas looked at Sandy, laughing, "I am sure I will pay for this later!"

Mr. Danforth came running up the path, out of breath. "You didn't think I was going to miss out on this nature walk, did you?"

Thomas looked back at Mr. Danforth, "Out of breath there, sir?"

Mr. Danforth grinned and winked at Thomas's little passenger.

As they headed down the trail, it was little Daniel that caught Mr. Danforth's eye. He watched him walking alone, pulling leaves off the trees as he passed them.

"Hey there, young man," he said, coming close. "Would you like to know the names of those trees?"

Daniel looked up and responded in a small voice, "I guess so."

Mr. Danforth began to tell Daniel about the trees and, strangely enough, Daniel began to open up, asking questions and commenting on things he found interesting. There was something about Daniel that tugged at Ted's heart. Maybe it was his dark hair, or the lost look on his face. Regardless of what it was exactly, he thought of Micah every time he looked at him.

※

145

While the main group was on their hike, Maggie had stayed behind with Peggy and Mr. Perry who had the daunting task of preparing lunch and the afternoon activities. They had only been working for about half an hour when Mr. Danforth walked in.

"I thought you were going to go on the nature hike, Dad?" Maggie commented with a frown.

"Oh, those young people have way too much energy for me. I came back after the first mile," Mr. Danforth laughed.

"Great," said Maggie, "here are some potatoes that need peeling." She handed him a vegetable peeler and a large pot of potatoes.

"Hmm … that nature trail is not looking so bad about now," said Mr. Danforth, glaring at the giant pot, then laughing again.

Maggie could not help but notice Mr. Danforth rubbing his right arm as if he was uncomfortable.

"Are you okay, Dad?" she asked with some concern. "Are you trying to get out of peeling potatoes?"

"Oh, this," giving his arm a hard rub. "I'm fine!"

"Well, you don't look fine," she said with a frown. "Actually, you seem to be sweating a little."

Mr. Danforth wiped his brow with a paper towel. "It is a little hot in here, Maggie, girl. I think I will go get some fresh air."

Mr. Danforth walked outside to get some fresh air and, after a few minutes, returned to the kitchen.

Maggie gave her father-in-law a stern look.

"Maggie … I'm fine," he said with a huff as he started working on the potatoes. "Would you quit fussing over me like a mother hen?"

The morning flew by, and before they knew it, the children were coming back from their long walk.

"Okay, everyone is all washed up and ready to eat. Hmm, something smells great," said Thomas.

One by one, the children sat down in the café. Maggie, Mr. Danforth, Peggy, and Mr. Perry began bringing out the food, and a feast was set out. Large bowls of potato salad, hotdogs, hamburgers, baked beans, and all the rest of the fixings, all graced the large tables.

Thomas attempted to get everyone's attention, clapping his hands together and standing, "So I think we should say grace and then we can dig in. Do I have any takers?"

Mr. Danforth raised his hand, much to the surprise of Maggie, Thomas, and Sandy. "Uh, Thomas," he said, clearing his throat, "if I may, I would like to say grace today."

Maggie could not remember the last time she heard Ted pray. Perhaps it had been even before Tom had passed. She just could not remember.

"Dear Lord," Mr. Danforth began, "thank You for all these wonderful children You have brought to us today. May You bless each one of them with a happy heart and a long and prosperous life. Lord, please bless the people who have opened up their hearts to be here to help. We just want to let You know that … we love You and that even though we do not say it enough, we know You love us. Amen."

Maggie wiped a tear from her eye and took Ted's hand in hers, saying quietly, "That was a great prayer, Dad."

Squeezing her hand in return, Mr. Danforth leaned over and whispered, "Thanks, Maggie. It's about time I let some of those unsaid prayers out, don't you think?"

That afternoon was filled with crafts, but soon enough dinner was served, and the children were tucked safely in bed after a story time around the fire. It truly was a great first day. Tomorrow they would take the children boating.

When everyone was asleep, Thomas laid in bed, holding Sandy and feeling quite satisfied about the day.

He thought about lunch and the surprise prayer, "Sandy, I didn't know Ted would offer to pray!"

Sandy lifted her head up from Thomas's chest, "Oh, I knew he had it in him. He has just been through so much."

Thomas kissed Sandy's forehead. "I guess you're right. It was nice. Really nice! I thank God for Mr. Danforth."

"Me, too, Thomas. Me, too," sighed Sandy as she drifted off to sleep.

Moments later, in the guest room, Ted Danforth looked up to see Micah standing near his bed.

"Oh, Micah," he sighed. "I have missed you so much!"

Micah did not say a word but took his grandfather's hand and began to lead him down a narrow, tree-lined path that had appeared.

Micah stopped suddenly and pointed to a man standing at the end of the path. "There's Daddy, Grandpa, see? Look!"

Straining to make out the figure, the shape of the man before him seemed to suddenly come into focus. Ted gasped as he could see that it was, indeed, his son.

"Tom!" Letting go of Micah's hand, Ted ran toward his son.

They embraced, neither wanting to ever let go. Ted took a deep breath, unable to believe that his arms were wrapped around his long, lost son. But when he opened his eyes, he was back in his room, and Tom was gone. He looked around, frantic, but Micah was nowhere to be found.

Suddenly, he started to cry uncontrollably, "Oh, God, please let me go back …"

As if God Himself came to sit by his bedside, he heard a whisper echo, "Soon, Ted … soon." Still crying, he slid back into his bed, taking comfort in the strange words, and falling back into a deep, peaceful sleep.

Chapter Fourteen

Goodbye, My Friend

Morning came fast, and smiling faces were everywhere as excited campers prepared for their boat ride and day of fishing. Gus had already made it down to the dock to make sure the life vests and fishing gear were ready, and now the boat just needed some passengers. The boat was a 24-foot pontoon. It was wheelchair accessible and had taken out many children with special needs in the past. It was not long before Gus could see Kelly, Mike, Sandy, Thomas, and Ted heading down the dock with the children. Smiling confidently, Sam was leading the group, as always.

"Morning, Gus," Thomas called. Gus, a man of few words, tipped his hat, offering a good morning with one quick nod.

"Are we ready for launch?" asked Thomas, as he placed a few coolers inside the boat.

Gus nodded again, "Yes, sir, we're ready!"

Sam wheeled onto the ramp that led onto the boat. Mike and Thomas lifted him out of the chair and seated him on a long bench on the deck to make it easier for him. Once the chair was on board, Thomas placed Sam back into his chair. Gus carefully fitted each child with a life vest as they sat down, one by one, on the bench.

Thomas looked at the group and, in his best pirate voice growled, "Arrrr, mates! Me-thinks Gus could give the crew safety instructions for the ship, since he is the most experienced ship's captain on the sea! And if he pays no mind, he had best walk the plank!"

All of the kids started laughing as their imaginations ran wild.

Gus playing along, nodded, and stepped to the center of the boat. In his own pirate voice, Gus yelled out, "Aye, children, this here is my boat! She is called the Queen An-gus, in case you are wonderin'. It is not a playground for rough neckin' around like wild bandits. You must sit still. No standin' or walkin' about. We'll be doin' some fishin' soon enough, so just be patient until we can get you a fishin' pole. Do ya have any questions?"

One little hand rose, and Thomas was surprised to see that it was Bethany. Gus smiled tenderly and walked over to her, waiting for her question. She motioned for him to come closer, so she could whisper in his ear. Gus leaned down, and Bethany got close to his head, whispering gently.

Clearing his throat, he answered Bethany in a low

tone, "Aye, you just let me know, and we'll turn the boat right around."

Bethany smiled and seemed satisfied with Gus's answer.

Sandy walked over to Gus, "Is there anything I can do to help?"

Gus looked at Sandy with a smile, "Ah, no, Ma'am. She just wanted to make sure that when she has to go, we can find her a little girl's room."

Sandy smiled, "I see … well, that was a really good question."

Old Gus looked around and replied, "Yes, ma'am, it was. Are there any more? Nope. Well, let's get a-movin'!"

The pontoon boat gently moved across the water until Gus found the perfect fishing spot. Thomas couldn't help but think of God and His beautiful world as he looked across the lake. The surroundings were breathtaking. The placid, shimmering water spread out across the lake, and wide-open spaces surrounded by tall pine trees could be seen along the banks. The gleam of sunlight reflecting off the water brought a smile to his face, and the gentle breeze filled his heart with peace.

When all the children were finally fitted with their poles, Thomas, Mike, Mr. Danforth, and Gus cast their lines out into the water with ease, instructing each child on the proper way to hold their pole. But a couple hours and a few bags of snacks went by without any bites, and the children were beginning to get restless, as no one had caught any fish.

Suddenly, Melanie stood up as she felt a tug on her

line. Before anyone could stop her, she climbed up onto the rail, leaning over to look past the edge of the boat. Within seconds, she was falling into the water with a horrendous scream. Mr. Danforth jumped into the water to retrieve the scared little girl. She wrapped her arms around his neck, still holding onto her pole with both hands. He lifted her up out of the lake as she spat water out of her mouth. Thomas and Mike pulled her back onto the boat.

Once she was back on deck, Sandy clutched her close, wrapping a blanket around her as Mr. Danforth was helped back up. Surprisingly, at the end of Melanie's line was a big, brown bass that weighed at least three pounds. It was certainly worth keeping. After the initial shock, Melanie appeared as if nothing was wrong. Grinning from ear to ear, he looked over at Mr. Danforth who was sitting on the bench, quite pale and dripping wet, and said, "I caught a fish!"

He looked at Melanie and couldn't help but smile, "Yup, you sure did!"

Thomas, looked down at Mr. Danforth and handed him a large towel. He had a concerned look was on his face and asked, "Are you okay, Ted?"

Mr. Danforth leaned his head up toward Thomas and whispered in his ear, "I think we need to head back now!"

Thomas looked at Gus, a feeling in his gut like something was very wrong, and instructed Gus to head home. Pulling up all the poles, the children sat back and enjoyed the speedy boat ride back to camp. To pass the time, Sandy and Kelly led the children in some old church songs.

Mr. Danforth closed his eyes and listened intently to the words. *"He's got the whole world in his hands; he's got the whole wide world, in his hands. He's got the whole world in his hands; he's got the whole world in his hands."*

Thomas looked over at Mr. Danforth who seemed to be sweating bullets. He moved closer, and Mr. Danforth suddenly did something so out of character for him that Thomas wouldn't have believed it if he hadn't experienced it himself. He threw his arm around Thomas and pulled him close.

"Thomas," he whispered, his voice harsh but certain. "I have to tell you this now. I have papers in the safe that will put you in charge of my company when I am gone. There may not be much time."

Thomas glanced at Mr. Danforth in shock, "But …"

"Shhhh!" he hissed, his brow furrowed and one hand clenched over his chest. "Let me finish, please. You have been like a son to me. Just promise me that you and Sandy will take care of Maggie. She will need you both. Once the boat lands, get the children off fast and take them to the café. Don't look back!"

Still unsure, but with a feeling of dread washing over him, tears came, unbidden, to Thomas's eyes. He sniffed, wiping his eyes with his sleeve while trying to hide his emotions for the sake of the children. Glancing over, Sandy could tell that something was wrong. Thomas looked at her, his eyes wide and terrified. He put his finger to his lips as if to say, "Shhh."

Once the boat pulled into the dock, Thomas stood slowly, telling everyone that they had to hurry to the café. Kelly and Mike lifted the wheelchair out, while Thomas lifted Sam, handing him to them. One by one, Sandy ushered the children off the boat. As she stepped onto the dock, Melanie turned suddenly, noticing that Mr. Danforth was still sitting in the boat. She broke free of the others and ran back onto the boat, wrapping her arms around Mr. Danforth's neck.

"I love you, sir ... thank you for saving me."

Mr. Danforth hugged her back, forcing a smile, "You are so welcome. Now run along ... the food is waiting!"

Melanie turned, skipping back, and leaving him alone with Gus and Thomas.

Thomas leaned close to Gus, shifting his eyes toward Ted, "Call 911. Now."

Gus looked at Mr. Danforth, realizing immediately how unwell he looked. He had seen that look many times, having been a medic in the Army, and he recognized the look on Ted's face. He pulled out his emergency phone and dialed 911.

"Yes," he said after a moment. "We have a man that may be having a heart attack at the Baker's place off Highway 210. We are at the boat dock. Please come right away!"

Mr. Danforth clutched at his chest, the pain getting progressively worse. Gus and Thomas sat with him, attempting to comfort him.

"It's going to be okay, Ted. Just hold on!" said Thomas, his voice shaking.

Mr. Danforth leaned up toward Thomas and whispered into his ear before falling back down, clenching his chest. He looked at Thomas again, his words coming in short breaths, "I'm going home, Thomas. Don't worry … I'm going home."

No sooner had the words left Mr. Danforth's mouth than he leaned back against the rail of the boat, closed his eyes, and was gone. Gus and Thomas glanced at each other with matching, horrified expressions. Standing, they quickly laid Mr. Danforth on the floor of the boat and frantically began CPR, not quitting until they heard the sirens and the EMS finally arrived.

Thomas knew in his heart that Mr. Danforth was gone, and he knew that there was nothing more they could do. As the EMTs did their jobs, checking Mr. Danforth's body and attempting resuscitation, Thomas looked up to see Maggie and Sandy making their way down to the dock, curious about the sirens from the ambulance.

When she saw the commotion on the boat, Maggie started running down the dock. "Oh, God, please no!" she cried, rushing toward her father-in-law.

Thomas held Maggie back as Sandy wrapped her arms around her, trying to comfort her. After a few minutes, the first paramedic looked up and said, "I am so sorry. He's gone."

Not very long after, Thomas and Maggie followed the ambulance in Thomas's car as it took Mr. Danforth's body to the local hospital. Everything was happening so fast that it seemed like a bad dream. Sandy walked back to the café, searching for the words to say. She walked in a daze, her thoughts blurred with sorrow and confusion. She would have to explain the sirens, and the fact that Mr. Danforth was no longer with them.

In the café, the children were busy eating, and there was an eerie silence over the room as Sandy walked in. Kelly and Mike headed over to her immediately, asking how Ted was. Sandy could barely look up, attempting to keep her face from the children so they would not see her grief.

"He's gone," she explained, trying to hide her tears. "He passed away!"

The shock on their faces was evident, and they both took a step back to sit down.

Sandy walked over to the table where the children were sitting, and asked if she could speak with them for a minute.

"Children, I have some bad news," she began, her voice wavering. "I know you heard all of the sirens and are probably wondering what was going on. Mr. Danforth is not going to be with us anymore this week. He, well, he was sick, and uh … had to go to the hospital."

She could not bring herself to tell them that he had died. Considering the circumstances, she thought that was best.

"Is he going to be okay?" asked Melanie. "He saved me, you know!"

A lump caught in Sandy's throat, and she tried not to cry, but she had no idea what to say to the little girl.

She looked at Melanie and said, "Well, honey, he is not hurting anymore. It's just that, well, he's gone home."

As the children continued their meal, Sandy tried to focus on what needed to be done. She knew she wouldn't be able stay the rest of the week with the children, but she did not want to cancel the camp.

Looking at Kelly and Mike, she asked, "Do you guys know anyone from the church that can replace us and help out with the camp for the rest of the week? I just … I need to be with Maggie and Thomas."

Mike spoke up first, "We had so many people volunteer for this week that we had to turn them away. Let me make some calls tonight, I'm sure we will have help by morning."

"Thanks, Mike. I will stay until the morning then."

The children spent the evening doing crafts, and soon it was time for bed. Sandy knew that Kelly and Mike could handle running the camp, as they had been a part of it for many years.

As she lay in bed after lights out, she prayed, "Dear Father, thank You for the time You gave us with Ted. I pray You will be with Maggie and comfort her. Please be with Thomas, too, Lord. I know this will hurt him very badly, as well. Please take care of us all."

Sandy closed her eyes, but sleep did not come. All she could see was Mr. Danforth walking her down the aisle at her wedding, his arm warm and comforting against hers, and his voice as he gave her away.

Chapter Fifteen

✳

Letting Go

Without much sleep, morning came slow and quiet, and the deep feeling of loss was heavier than ever on Sandy's heart. She had been sitting out on the boat dock most of the night, waiting for the sun to rise and hoping Thomas would call soon. When her phone rang suddenly, her stomach seemed to roll, making her feel queasy and dizzy. Not only did Sandy have to deal with this horrible loss, but she had also not felt well, her body tired and achy and nauseous throughout the night. She did not want to worry Thomas, however, and quickly pushed it to the back of her mind as she answered.

"Hello? Thomas, are you okay? I have been so worried about you and Maggie."

In a soft, forlorn voice, he told her that Maggie was so distraught that she wanted to be left alone. He had stayed at Mr. Danforth's office all night.

His voice cracking, he told Sandy that he had found the papers Mr. Danforth had left him. He felt guilty for looking for them, and even for reading them. He also knew they had a lot of important information in them, not to mention that many people depended on Mr. Danforth and would have to be told of his passing and what to expect. There would have to be a news release, a board meeting, and many other details that would need to be worked out quickly.

Thomas went on to share with her that he had found some legal papers that stated Mr. Danforth's desires when it came to his death. He did not want a funeral and had even requested that no one have a memorial service.

"Doesn't that sound just like him, Sandy? He wants to leave this earth quickly and with little fuss. He requested that his body be cremated! I am not sure about this at all. Cremated? But, that's what he wants."

"I know, honey," said Sandy tenderly. "You have to respect his wishes."

"Sandy, there is more. I'm not really sure how to say this. His dying wish was that I take over the company. He whispered this in my ear as he was dying, Sandy. He told me that he had papers stating this. I found them last night!" Thomas said, and Sandy could hear the tears in his voice.

She tried to comfort him, "Honey, I know. I am so sorry. But you can't feel guilty! This was what Mr. Danforth wanted. He would be proud that you are taking care of the business. He learned to love you like the son he lost. What greater honor is there than that?"

"I know. It's just that I want to grieve so badly, but I

can't even do that! There is so much to do."

Sandy looked up to see a pair of cars pulling up in the driveway. Two young couples got out of the cars, and she immediately recognized them from church.

"Thomas, our relief is here from the church. I am coming to see you. Don't worry. Kelly and Mike can handle everything here. I'll see you soon. I love you."

Sandy was feeling more and more nauseated as the morning wore on, but she put on her best face. She walked up to the new volunteers, welcoming and thanking them for coming on such short notice. Offering them breakfast, they headed to the café. Soon after, Mike brought out her things and placed them in the trunk of her car. With tears in her eyes once again, she said good-bye to the group and drove away.

Knowing the children were taken care of gave her a lot of peace, but her thoughts were moving at such a fast pace that it was quite difficult to keep the nausea at bay. Suddenly, an intense revelation filled her thoughts, and she almost slammed on the brakes. *Good Lord, I may be pregnant!*

As she drove, she pushed the thought aside, not wanting to think about anything except the problem at hand, and not really believing that it was true to begin with. She arrived at Mr. Danforth's office to find Thomas staring out the giant window. He appeared deep in thought and didn't hear Sandy come in. She closed the door carefully behind her and walked quietly, not wanting to disturb him.

"Thomas," Sandy said softly as she placed her hand

on the back of his shoulder.

As Thomas slowly turned around to face her, she could see the pain in his blood-shot eyes, evidence of his sleepless night of crying.

"Oh, Thomas, honey, I am so sorry."

Thomas embraced her suddenly, wrapping his arms around her tightly and letting out a harsh sob, "I am going to miss him so much. I will never be able to fill his shoes."

Sandy held him for a long time, saying nothing, until he gently released her from his embrace.

"Thomas, God has you here for a reason. You have to trust Him. It's going to be all right."

She watched him stand tall, trying to take in her words and find comfort in them.

"If you're okay," she continued, "let's go see Maggie and check on her."

Thomas agreed, wiping his face with both hands. "I made hotel reservations for a few days, so we can be near Maggie, and I can take care of things here at the office."

Sandy nodded, wrapping her arms around her husband once again, "That sounds like a good idea, love."

Later that morning, Thomas and Sandy arrived at Maggie's house, which had been Mr. Danforth's luxurious home. Maggie and Micah had lived there since Tom passed away. The two of them had used most of the house, while Ted kept only a bedroom and his study in the far left wing for himself. Now it was hers alone. The house was located in the rather well off part of town, and was a beautiful sight. Pulling up to the large iron gates, Thomas pressed the intercom button to alert Maggie that someone was at the gate.

"Hello?" asked Maggie.

"Maggie, it's Sandy and me. Would you let us in so we can talk?"

There was a long pause before the gates began to open, allowing them access. Thomas pulled the car around the driveway to the front of the house.

Maggie was standing out front, her arms folded over her chest, looking down at the ground. Sandy got out and rushed to her. Putting her arms around her, she hugged her tenderly.

Maggie began to cry, "I can't believe he's gone, Sandy. He was all I had left in this world. I just don't understand."

Sandy continued to hold Maggie and allowed her to cry. Thomas moved closer, standing beside Sandy and wiping his own tears away.

"Please come in. I sent the staff home. I just needed to be alone," Maggie explained between sobs.

Sandy and Thomas looked at each other, realizing that they were all suffering from the same pain. No words or clichés seemed appropriate. Deep down they knew it would take more than time for them to get over this tragedy. It just wasn't that easy to heal. After all, how much pain can one person endure in such a short period of time?

Maggie looked at them, "You know, he didn't want a

165

memorial, funeral, or anything."

Thomas looked at her, "Yes, that's what I read. It's okay, though, Maggie. We will always have him right here."

He tapped his chest, right over his heart, and tried to offer her a comforting smile. When it failed, a thought occurred to him, and he decided to ask about something he'd been considering.

"You know, I have been thinking about something. I am not sure if this is the time to mention it, but what would you girls think about taking a trip to China?"

Both women looked up, surprised and perplexed. They exchanged a glance.

"What?" Sandy asked. This wasn't a conversation she'd been expecting.

"I know this may seem too soon after Ted's passing, but there is something I have to tell you," Thomas said. "I'm not sure how many people know this, or even if you do, Maggie, but Ted has been supporting a small orphanage in China for the last ten years. He has been almost their sole support. He has taken a trip every year, personally delivering them the money needed to keep the orphanage running. He would also attend some business meetings when he was there. I happened to find his calendar and he had a flight booked for next week. A notation was made to withdraw funds to take, to give to the orphanage. I have no doubt they are waiting for his visit and the donation."

Maggie started laughing and crying at the same time, "Leave it to Ted. He is not even going to allow us time to grieve for him. You know I had him cremated this morning. I placed his ashes with his beloved wife, at his request. It is hard to not have some memorial, but I have to follow his request. And I know this would be how he wanted to be honored."

As they walked inside, she confided that she had known that he supported an orphanage, but he always handled it privately and never asked for her to be involved.

"He never really talked about it," she said. "It was as if he didn't want anyone to know the good he was doing. I remember one time I caught him looking at this picture. It was a picture of him and a little girl named Ching Lan. He told me he had watched her grow up in the orphanage since she was two years old. The picture was taken when she was nine. When the horrible earthquake happened a few years ago, the orphanage suffered a lot of damage. Ted flew out right away. Sadly, Ching Lan died with three other children. He spent quite a bit of time and money rebuilding the facility and providing supplies. Since resources in that area were very limited and the government would do little in spite of his many efforts, he helped many people in the quake area."

Thomas stood in awe, quite shocked at this information concerning his former boss.

"This must have happened right before I came on board. I did see a picture of Ted and this little girl, but I had no idea who she was or where she was from. I had assumed it was a client's child."

Sandy grabbed Maggie's hand suddenly, "Let's go to

China! Please?"

Maggie turned away from the couple, thinking about the idea. For a moment, she gazed at a family photo on the wall. After about twenty seconds, she turned back quickly and shouted with excitement, "Yes, let's go to China!"

Thomas smiled at the beaming ladies, "Okay, then. I will book two more tickets. We are going to China!"

For a few minutes, their hearts felt an overwhelming rush of joy and peace. With this hope-filled plan, the sting of losing Mr. Danforth did not seem to hurt quite as badly. Now they were faced with the challenge of carrying on his legacy.

Suddenly, Sandy covered her mouth with her hand and ran to the nearest bathroom.

Chapter Sixteen

❋

Expect the Unexpected

At Maggie's insistence, Thomas and Sandy spent the night in a lovely room at the Danforth estate. Lying in the plush bed, Thomas could tell that something was bothering Sandy. She had been quiet for most of the evening, and she did not look herself.

"Honey, what's wrong?" he asked. "You don't look so well tonight."

Sandy looked up at Thomas and took a deep breath, "I did not want to tell you, but … I think I'm pregnant."

Thomas sat straight up in bed, "What … when … how? I mean, not how, of course, but … *what*?"

Sandy laughed, "I have been feeling nauseous a lot lately, with a little cramping, too. I only realized it yesterday, but everything happened with Ted, and I felt like I should wait to tell you. But now that we are going to China, I guess I should take a pregnancy test."

"You think?" he teased, a silly grin on his face.

Reaching over to hug her, Thomas was beyond happy, "I can't believe this, honey! You—I mean, *we*—are going to have a baby!"

Later, while Sandy was asleep, Thomas got up during the night and headed to the nearest store to get a pregnancy test. He wanted to be ready the next morning when Sandy woke up. He was hoping for good news, and just couldn't wait.

When morning came, they ate breakfast, waiting for Maggie to come down from her room. When Maggie came into the kitchen, she immediately paused and stared at them with a strange expression.

"You two look like you've swallowed a canary. What gives?"

Holding up their positive pregnancy test, Thomas and Sandy shouted in unison, "We're having a baby!"

Maggie gasped and started jumping up and down, "Oh, my goodness, we're going to have a baby! This is so great!"

Within moments, Sandy gripped her stomach, crying out in pain. A hot, searing pain ripped through her abdomen, and it was all she could do not to scream.

"Honey, what's wrong?" asked Thomas, suddenly scared.

"Call 911. Now!" Sandy said, gasping through tears.

Maggie raced for her phone and called an ambulance. Sandy was young and healthy, and they figured that she was only about four weeks pregnant, so there certainly were no indications that her pregnancy could be at risk. But as she crouched over in her seat, clenching her body in tears, they were immediately worried.

Thomas and Maggie followed the ambulance to the Emergency Room. Sandy was quickly wheeled in, and a doctor was by her side almost immediately. After a few tests, he determined that she was suffering from an ectopic, or tubal, pregnancy and that her fallopian tube had ruptured. She was rushed into surgery, where they were able to stop the bleeding and fix the problem, but by morning she had lost the baby.

Sandy was devastated. Although it had come a little early, the idea of having a baby had lifted her spirits and made her feel alive with hope. But now everything seemed to be rushing at her from all sides. Ted's death had only been a few days ago, and now this? But there was further bad news. Because of the incident, Sandy was left with little hope of getting pregnant again. The other tube was blocked and, though the doctors said there was always a slight chance and explained that she could always try other means, Sandy was left empty and depressed.

Although it hadn't been formally planned, the three of them decided that the trip to China would have to be postponed a couple of weeks so that Sandy could recover, but it was not long before she was up and moving around again.

"Thomas, I am so sorry," Sandy said, a few weeks later, her voice choked with tears.

She was sitting at the dinner table, her eyes blurry and unfocused as she watched Thomas move around the kitchen.

"Sorry? Honey ... I don't understand," he said as he finished cleaning up after dinner.

"I may not be able to give you children," Sandy said, her voice weak and broken.

Drying his hands, he pulled her close, "Then God has other plans, and we will trust in him, like we have many other times."

That day, they made their plans to go to China with Maggie. They had good work there, and children to help, and they didn't want to put it off any longer.

❈

After another few weeks, the morning finally came when the group would be flying to Beijing.

"Thomas, do you have the tickets?" asked Sandy, locking the front door behind her.

Thomas looked back at Sandy, and flashed the tickets in front of her face, "Of course, I do. Doors all locked?"

"Yep!" said Sandy, pulling her suitcase behind her. "Oh, Thomas, I am so excited! I have such a good feeling about this trip. There is a joy that is just welling up in my soul, and I can't explain it!"

Thomas stopped, looking at Sandy. He thought about everything they'd been through, good and bad, and remembered suddenly how blessed he was just to have her.

"I love to see you like this, Sandy," he said with a soft

grin. "You are so beautiful when you're smiling."

Gus ran up to the truck, just in time, "Mornin'! Mr. Mitchell, let me get those suitcases for you!"

"Thanks, Gus! I guess I don't need to leave you any instructions. I mean, you have been running this place without me for a very long time."

Gus looked up, smiling, "No, sir, don't you and Sandy worry. I gotcha covered!"

Sandy and Thomas waved goodbye to Gus and started to drive away. Thomas took a quick look in the rear view mirror to see Gus still waving goodbye. *What a blessing this man has been,* he thought to himself.

It was not long before they pulled up to the ornate gate of Mr. Danforth's estate. Surprisingly, Maggie was waiting outside already with suitcases in hand. Sandy rolled down the window.

"Maggie, are you a bit excited?" she asked, laughing.

Maggie put her suitcase in the trunk and hopped into the back seat. With a large grin she said, *"Wo men qu ba!"*

Sandy and Thomas turned around in their seats to stare at her with raised eyebrows.

"What did you just say?" asked Thomas, laughing.

Maggie repeated it once more, slower. She could barely contain her laughter. Giggling, she said, "It means, 'let's go,' in Chinese."

Sandy smiled, "Well then, *wo men qu ba*!"

The fourteen-hour flight was smooth with no delays, and they arrived in Beijing early the next day. The time difference threw them off a little, but they had fun trying to work out the numbers and time zone changes, and they took a lot of naps. Although there had been an in-flight meal, by the time they stepped off the plane, they were all very hungry. The first thing they saw in the terminal was a colorful noodle shop, and Thomas encouraged Sandy and Maggie to grab something there, since they had no idea how long it would be until they would be able to eat again.

Before leaving the States, Thomas had called the local office in Beijing and arranged for transportation and a place to stay. The head of the office there, Mr. Jim Reinhart, would be picking them up. He had lived in China for over five years and was one of their top-notch engineers.

Around noon, not long after they took their last slurp of noodles, a man approached their table.

"Mr. Mitchell?"

They looked up and acknowledged the middle-aged man with dark hair, a professional smile, and a slight British accent extending his hand to shake.

"Yes," Thomas said, accepting his hand. "I'm Thomas Mitchell, and you must be Mr. Reinhart. So nice to meet you. This is my wife, Sandy, and Mr. Danforth's daughter in-law, Maggie."

"Please, call me Jim," Mr. Reinhart said, looking at Maggie with a frown. "I am so sorry to hear of Mr. Danforth's passing. Please accept my utmost condolences.

He was truly a wonderful man."

Maggie's sorrow was evident, but she gave him a small smile. "Yes, he was. Thank you," she said, softly.

Mr. Reinhart continued, "Maggie, you may not remember me, but I was taking some time off in the good ole USA a few years back, and I met you and your son."

Maggie looked more closely at his face, but did not recognize him.

"I'm sorry," she said. "I don't quite remember."

Mr. Reinhart laughed, "Don't fret about that. I have a forgettable face, I am afraid! Here, let me help you with your baggage. I have the car out front. The village is almost two hours outside of the city, and they are expecting us before an early dinner."

With Jim's assistance, Thomas, Sandy, and Maggie, loaded their luggage into the boot of a black company sedan. Maggie and Sandy sat in the back seat while Thomas sat up front with Jim.

Attempting to make small talk, Mr. Reinhart looked through the rear view mirror at Maggie. "Ms. Danforth, how is your son? I believe he was just a small lad when I last saw him."

Maggie looked at Sandy and then Thomas, unable to answer Mr. Reinhart. Thomas stepped in to save Maggie from having to answer.

"Mr. Reinhart, it has actually been a very difficult year on all of us. Maggie lost Micah to cancer this past year."

Jim's face turned noticeably red, his brow furrowing with sorrow and embarrassment for bringing up such a hurtful subject. "Oh ... I am beyond words. Please forgive me! Please forgive me, one and all."

Maggie reached forward and touched Mr. Rinehart's shoulder, "You didn't know, Jim. It's alright."

An awkward silence fell then as they made their way out of the busy city.

After a time, Mr. Reinhart broke the silence, "We are heading to a small village just outside of Tianjin, where the orphanage is located. I have actually spent quite some time there when not working. It's very lovely."

Suddenly curious, Sandy asked, "Mr. Reinhart, did you know Ching Lan, the little girl that Mr. Danforth cared for?"

Jim broke into a big smile, "I surely did, and what a beautiful child she was. Sadly, as you know, the earthquake took her little life too soon, and a couple of other children as well. Mr. Danforth spent a lot of money reconstructing the orphanage after that quake. It was a great loss for him. He loved her so."

Thomas spoke up next, "How many children live there now, Jim?"

He glanced at Thomas, "Well, there are 31 children total, with the addition of another child just this past week. The strangest thing happened, actually. Ching Lan's mother showed up on the doorstep with a newborn baby boy. She claims that an American businessman is the father. Like Ching Lan, she has no way to care for him and would be shunned by her family because she is not married, and the child is half-Caucasian."

"How awful, Jim," said Maggie in a soft voice.

Jim looked at Maggie through the rear view mirror. "Yes … it is a sad affair. We can only hope he can be adopted quickly and not spend his life in the orphanage."

Sandy placed her hand on Thomas's shoulder. He turned around to look at her, and it seemed as if both were thinking the same thing, though only time would tell.

"Mr. Reinhart, how did you get involved with the orphanage? I mean, being an engineer and all?" asked Thomas, turning back to him.

Mr. Rinehart smiled once again, "Oh, I am so glad you asked. It is my favorite story to tell, actually. Mr. Danforth sent me to China five years ago under the condition that I would oversee the orphanage for him. Mr. Danforth said that it would not be a huge undertaking. It was supposed to be just making sure funds were delivered, supplies were bought and delivered, and I would keep him abreast of the comings and goings.

"I was not thrilled at first, I have to tell you. I am an engineer with no children of my own. My wife passed away ten years ago, and I had no purpose but to work twenty-four hours a day. Life became boring if I ever took time off for myself. I didn't know how to enjoy life or feel what it's like to have any other purpose but my own. Mr. Danforth hired me six years ago and, not long after, asked who would like to work in China. I, of course, was the first to volunteer. I was running away, I guess you could say. I was willing to take on added duties to my already busy schedule but was not particularly thrilled about it.

Taking care of an orphanage was not the kind of work I was looking for.

"I protested a few times, but after going to the orphanage, it was not long before my heart was captivated. Please, don't laugh, but they even have a special name for me."

Thomas looked over at him again, "What might that be, Jim?"

Mr. Reinhart once again turned slightly red, "They call me *Bobo*. It means *uncle*. You see, they've considered Mr. Danforth to be a father, so I am the *uncle* on his side."

As the words were said, the sedan was suddenly filled with laughter, forever breaking the awkward silence that had come before.

Chapter Seventeen

✻

Great Expectations

No one knew what to expect as Thomas, Sandy, Maggie, and Mr. Reinhart pulled up to the orphanage. The visitors were pleasantly surprised at the quaint, wood-framed house, standing alone among the trees. It had a peaceful and serene feel to it, with mountains surrounding the land of the orphanage like a protective barrier. They could already hear the joyous laughter of the children running around the grounds, playing. Watching the children from the car, Mr. Reinhart began to explain the unfamiliar game that the children appeared to be playing.

"Oh, look! They are playing 'The Eagle and the Chicks'. Look over there. You see one child is the eagle and one is the hen? All the other children are chicks. That young girl over there must be the hen as the little chicks are lining up behind her," he said, pointing out each player.

"She has to keep the eagle from taking one of her chicks."

The group smiled, enjoying the sight.

"It appears as if the eagle has tagged one of the little chicks," said Maggie, giggling.

The children stopped running as they noticed the strangers in the car. Curious and shy, they huddled together, whispering, and slowly made their way to the porch.

"Oh, they are so adorable!" said Sandy, smiling, as they got out of the car.

Mr. Reinhart stepped forward. "Hello, my little chicks!" he said in Chinese.

Suddenly, sounds of laughter poured from the little ones as they came running up to him, surrounding him with hugs and greetings.

"Bobo," they said excitedly in both Chinese and English, "Where have you been?"

Mr. Reinhart responded in fluent Chinese and began introducing Thomas, Sandy, and Maggie. The children were so happy and excited to have visitors, and they took to them immediately, grabbing their hands and leading them to the porch.

About that time, the house caretakers, an elegant older woman named Chen and a tall, homely man named Daiyu, came out of the house. Bowing in traditional local style, the woman said in a soft voice, "Welcome, Mr. Reinhart!"

Her English was very good, and she quickly ushered everyone toward the house. At the door, they each were instructed to remove their shoes. Off to the side was a simple shoe rack, loaded with slippers for the visitors to use inside. The children sat on the floor, removing their shoes obediently, and placing slippers on their feet. One by one, they made their way inside.

Thomas grabbed Sandy's hand, "Do you smell that?"

Sandy took a deep breath and caught a warm scent from inside. She smiled, "Doesn't it smell wonderful?"

Inside, Chen motioned for the guests to sit down. Dinner was prepared on large, short-legged round tables around the dining room. The children all sat on pillows around the short-legged tables. They sat quietly, as if waiting on permission to eat. The tables were already adorned with large bowls of food such as rice, egg flower soup, shrimp and fish, vegetables, and fruit resting on large rotating wooden bases.

Daiyu looked at Mr. Reinhart, "Please, sir, will you say grace?"

Jim bowed his head and offered a prayer in English, "Dear Lord God, thank You for bringing our friends safely to us. May this visit bring many blessings and honor to You."

Chen looked around at the children and nodded her head, letting them know it was time to eat.

As they began to feast, there was a sudden wail of crying. With all the excitement, the lone crib against the wall had gone unnoticed. Chen got up quickly, picking up a tiny baby with gentle, delicate motions.

"Thomas, look …" Sandy whispered.

Without really thinking about it, Sandy got up from the table and stood next to Chen. Her heart was beating fast, filled with emotions that even she did not understand.

"May I hold him, Chen?" Sandy asked, her voice almost a whisper.

Chen smiled and handed the tiny infant to her.

The child was almost two weeks old. He had shimmering black hair, fair skin, and soft dark eyes.

Sandy looked at the baby with intense compassion. She felt as if he had been waiting for her to come along and get him. How could that even be possible?

Looking at Mr. Reinhart, Chen explained, "This is poor Ching Lan's baby brother. His mother left him when he was only two days old. He is a fragile little thing and so very young. We haven't even named him yet."

Maggie and Jim stood up from the table and moved closer to Sandy, admiring the adorable baby.

"Thomas, look at him. He is so cute." Sandy's face glowed with love for the infant.

Thomas, who had been playing with a couple of boys at the table, looked up and made his way toward her. Without a thought, Sandy handed him the baby.

"Uh, Sandy, I haven't held a …"

But the baby was already in his arms, and Thomas's words were cut short. He looked at the precious little one, and he was immediately moved. Just like Sandy, the precious infant in his arms melted his heart.

"He is so tiny … look at his little fingers and toes," murmured Thomas, thoughtfully.

Chen and Daiyu looked at each other. "I believe our prayers have been answered," Chen spoke in Chinese.

Mr. Reinhart, understanding Chinese, realized instantly what Chen and Daiyu were thinking. He raised an eyebrow, wondering at the ways lives were so often brought together.

With a polite smile, Chen spoke in English this time, "Please, let us finish our meal. We will speak after dinner."

The meal went fast, the visitors enjoying the flavorful, traditional fare. Afterward, the children cleared their tables and tucked themselves into bed after a group prayer. Sandy and Thomas found their obedience to be truly remarkable.

Once the little ones were asleep, the adults gathered in the sitting area, sharing a large pot of tea. Mr. Reinhart was the first to speak.

"Chen and Daiyu, I have money for the orphanage, but I have some bad news to share with you. Mr. Danforth passed away recently. However, he has put his trust in all of us to take care of the orphanage, just as he did for all these years."

Sorrow covered the faces of the orphanage caretakers.

"We are so sorry. He was a great man and very good to us," said Chen, her voice soft and polite.

Maggie spoke up after being very quiet the whole evening, "May I say, I would love to be a part of the orphanage in any way that I can be of assistance."

Thomas and Sandy looked at each other, rather surprised. They were not sure what Maggie meant.

"I don't have anything now to keep me in the States," Maggie explained. "As soon as I stepped out of that car, I felt the Lord telling me I am supposed to be here. For how long, I don't know, but I feel that I should be here."

Daiyu looked at Chen, and they both smiled again. There was no need for a translator, and the language barrier between the group didn't seem to have any effect as they both said in perfect English, "Praise God in Heaven."

Mr. Reinhart looked at Maggie, a look of surprise and interest on his face, "Do you mean you want to stay here and work with the orphanage?"

Maggie laughed, "Yes, that is exactly what I mean! I have not felt like I had a purpose since Micah passed, and then dad. This may be my new purpose."

Sandy heard the baby crying and, without thought, quickly got up, not waiting for Chen or Daiyu. Thomas followed behind her as she made her way to the crib.

Looking at Thomas, Sandy asked softly, "Are you thinking what I am thinking?"

He kissed her on the cheek gently and brought his lips to her ear, whispering so no one would hear them, "I think we should adopt him, if we can."

Sandy could hardly contain herself and had to force her voice into a whisper, "Really, Thomas? Oh, yes! I knew the minute I held him that he was ours!"

The couple turned around, noticing with a start that everyone in the room was watching them.

Thomas looked at Chen, "Chen, how hard would it be to start the paperwork for Sandy and me to adopt … uh …" looking at Sandy, he thought about what Chen had said about the infant not having a name, and groped for one for a moment. Suddenly they both knew exactly what it should be, and said, together, "Micah?"

Maggie jumped up, almost in shock, "Micah? You are going to name him Micah?"

Sandy suddenly felt a little nervous, wondering if they had upset Maggie by being so presumptuous about naming the baby. She wondered if they should have been more sensitive to her feelings first.

"Maggie," she said slowly, "we would never want to hurt you. Please, if this is too painful …"

Maggie rushed to her and threw her arms around the three of them, "Hurt me? Oh, no, I am so thrilled! That would be wonderful!"

"Maggie, I would like to share something with you that we learned when Sandy was pregnant." Thomas sounded serious, and everyone stopped to listen. "I was looking at Sandy's book of baby names, and out of curiosity, I looked up the name 'Micah'. It is of Hebrew origin and means 'Who is like God?'. I'm not saying that Micah represented God, but he's a reminder of how much God is in control of our circumstances and how little we are. Just look at how he used Micah to bring all of us together."

Maggie smiled at Thomas and gave him another hug, realizing for the first time how much he felt like a brother to her. "Thank you for sharing that with me, Thomas."

Chen and Daiyu stood and joined them, watching the group with a smile. With Jim's help, Chen explained, "We will start the papers tonight. It will take some time, but there should not be any problem since the mother has given up her rights, not to mention that the child is half Chinese and half American."

Thomas looked at Mr. Reinhart. "Jim, I guess Sandy and I need to find a place to stay for a few weeks while we wait. Do you have any ideas?"

Jim was speechless. So much had happened in such a short amount of time that he had to pause a moment to gather his thoughts. His head was swimming. *Only my God,* he thought, *only my God could do all of this!*

"I have a large flat in the city," he said. "You, Sandy, and Maggie are welcome to stay with me. I would be honored and would certainly enjoy the company."

Maggie spoke up, "I think I will be staying here with Chen and Daiyu, so there's no need to worry about me!"

Sandy looked down at Micah, already sleeping as she held him. Warm and smooth in her arms, she suddenly felt as if holding him were the most natural thing in the world, and she never wanted to stop. "I can't leave him now, Thomas," she said. "I will stay here, too!"

Thomas glanced at her in surprise, "We are?"

Sandy looked up at him with a sheepish smile and gestured to the infant, "You can stay with Jim if you want, but how can you possibly be separated from him for even one moment?"

He looked at Mr. Reinhart, "Well, it looks like we will not need a place after all."

"Chen, do you have room for all of us?" asked Sandy.

Chen replied slowly, thinking about it, "Yes, of course. I have two extra rooms, and we would be most honored."

Jim looked around at everyone, a little amazed, "Well, I should be leaving then. I think I will say goodnight, but I will see you all in the morning. Thomas, I can pick you up, and we can go over some details at the office, if that is good for you."

Thomas shook his hand, "Yes, Jim, that would be great. Thank you for everything!"

After a round of goodbyes, Mr. Reinhart left, and the rest of the evening was spent discussing the adoption, as well as Maggie's decision to stay at the orphanage. When it was far past their bedtime, the guests were shown to their separate rooms and prepared for bed. Although they had known they wanted to adopt Micah from the first time they laid eyes on him, they did not want to seem too pushy, so when Chen mentioned that Micah had bonded with her and slept in her room, they did not argue.

Everyone was settled in for the night when Thomas heard a slight knock on the door.

It was Daiyu, a worried frown overtaking his face, "Please sir, the baby is sick!"

"Sandy!" Thomas whispered loudly, shaking her. "Wake up. The baby is sick!"

They threw on their robes and followed Daiyu to the living room where Chen was rocking Micah gently.

"He is very sick," Chen said, her voice quiet but obviously worried. " He is very warm. Please, you look at him?"

Sandy had told the women earlier that she was a children's doctor, and would be glad to give each child a physical during their trip. A medical program had been in place for quite a few years thanks to Mr. Danforth, and Dr. Huang came once a year to give the children their immunizations, yearly hearing and vision tests, and offering medical care should a problem arise. But, just in case, Sandy was more than happy to give them checkups while she was there.

Micah was only a couple of weeks old but had been examined by Dr. Huang the week he had come to the orphanage.

Fear gripping her heart, Sandy found her bag, pulling out some supplies. She used her stethoscope first. She could tell Micah had a slight rattle in his lungs, which indicated that he might have an upper respiratory infection. A quick temperature check showed a fever as well.

Attempting to explain in non-professional terms and simple English, Sandy said, "Chen, we need to call Dr. Huang! I don't have the medication Micah needs. I think he has an infection in his chest."

Chen nodded in agreement, handing Micah to her, "You care for him. You are the doctor."

Sandy looked at Thomas, "I need to get his fever down. We need to run a cool bath, but he is not going to like it."

Thomas drew a cool bath in the sink and placed a towel in the bottom. Sandy removed Micah's sleeper, noting how small and frail he appeared. Much to her surprise, he did not fuss very much during his bath, except for a few muttered cries when the water first covered his small body.

Chen made the phone call to Dr. Huang and let them know he would be there in the morning. It was getting late, and Sandy could tell Chen was exhausted. She would have to get up with the other children quite early, and Sandy didn't want her to suffer for this.

"Chen, please go to sleep, I can stay up with Micah! That is, if you are okay with me stepping in."

A smile spread across Chen's face, "Yes, that will be fine. You are going to be the mother. You need to take care of him."

Sandy looked at Thomas, who would also be waking up early to head to the office with Mr. Reinhart, "You go get a couple hours of sleep, too. Micah and I are fine. Go on to bed."

Thomas looked at Sandy with such love in his heart. Micah was in her arms, wrapped in a light blanket, as she was rocking him to sleep. There were only a few hours left of the night, and with the time change from home, Thomas was especially tired. He would need as much sleep as possible before going to work in the morning.

"Okay, if you are sure."

Kissing her on the forehead, he said, "'Night, my love. Good night, my little man."

Sandy rocked Micah in the dark, the moon shining through the window, casting a light upon the child's face.

"Father," she prayed, "thank You for our son. I stand amazed at the way you have led us here. I never dreamed we would be adopting a baby. Father God, please bless Maggie as she stays here to work in the orphanage. Bless this home and keep them safe. Amen."

Chapter Eighteen

✻

Final Days

The days flew by, and before they knew it, two weeks had passed. It was now time to say their goodbyes. The adoption had gone smoothly, and Thomas and Sandy had signed the final papers the day before. They could now take their son home. They felt surprisingly comfortable leaving Maggie in Tianjin. It was obvious that a friendship was building between her and Mr. Reinhart.

That day, Maggie and Jim drove Thomas, Sandy, and little baby Micah to the airport. With tearful hugs and goodbyes, Maggie said, "I want lots of pictures of Micah, you two!"

Sandy squeezed her friend with tears in her own eyes, "Of course! And we will plan on making a trip back, soon! Don't forget, I am only a phone call away."

Thomas shook Jim's hand, "Take good care of Maggie.

She's like family."

Mr. Reinhart smiled, "I will do my best. Don't worry."

Sandy, Thomas, and the new baby boarded the plane. Hearts were torn at the separation, but deep down they were excited about going home to get their lives moving with their new family.

Once in their seats, Thomas took his wife's hand, offering a quiet prayer, "Lord, thank You for Micah and the wonderful blessings You have given us. Let us always trust in Your provision and Your plan."

Ten years later ...

Remember God's playbook?
His everlasting plan?
Let's peek into the future and
see the journey that has unfolded
in the lives of our friends.

Through the years, Thomas continued to run Mr. Danforth's company with the same compassion and inspiration of his mentor. Sandy finished her residency and opened her own free clinic, relying on their community and support from their local church to help those in need, especially children.

Sandy and Thomas ended up adopting three more children from China, a little girl named Aaryn and a pair of twins, Callie and Camila. They still ran the camp every summer. Over time, Gus asked Jesus into his heart, and never missed a Sunday service. Sadly, he was now an old man and could no longer work the way he did in the past. But Thomas and Sandy had grown to love him dearly and moved him into their house, as they did not want him to be alone.

Maggie and Jim got married after a year and continued to work in China. They never had or adopted any children of their own but believed all the children at the orphanage were theirs. Maggie became fluent in Mandarin Chinese and remained very happy with her life there.

"Micah, get your sisters. It's time to leave, or we'll be late!"

Thomas grabbed the last of the suitcases, putting them into the van.

Sandy looked over at him, "I can't wait to see Maggie! I can't believe it's been two years since our last visit!"

Thomas pulled her into a hug, "Me, too. And I know the children are excited to see their homeland again!"

They all piled into the van and headed off, giddy and excited about the trip to China. The girls chattered in the back as everyone prepared themselves for the long journey, discussing the things they were excited for and what they would like to do.

All of a sudden, Micah, now eleven, spoke up, "Dad? Have I told you I love you lately?"

Thomas was taken by surprise, "No, son, I don't think I have heard that lately."

Then Aaryn chimed in, "Me, too, Daddy!"

Callie and Camila spoke next, in unison, "Us, too, Daddy!"

Thomas was suddenly overtaken with emotion. Tears began to run down his face. Pulling the car over, he turned around to see his beautiful children smiling at him.

"I love you, too!" he said, his smile growing as he wiped his tears away. "Remember the love song I used to sing to all of you? Can we sing it together?"

Everyone agreed and quickly chimed in together.

"I love you higher than the heavens
and the stars in the sky,
deeper than the oceans
and the mountains so high,
longer than a river flowing
from a point unknown,
forever means forever,
every time we sing this song!"

Looking at Sandy, Thomas said in a soft voice, "Have I told you lately how much I love you?"

Sandy squeezed his hand, "You tell me every day!"

He put the van in gear, "So, does anyone want to go to China?"

From the back of the van, the children cheered.

With a smile that still warmed his heart after all these years, Sandy leaned over and whispered, "I wonder what God's next move will be?"

Thomas laughed, pulling back onto the road, "Only our God knows!"

Authors

Kevin Kruise and Kimberly Kruise Thompson
Brother and Sister

About the Authors

When **Kimberly Kruise Thompson** and brother **Kevin Kruise** were growing up, they spent many days writing songs and poetry and singing together. When they were barely five, their mother would sit them on the piano bench next to her and teach them to sing together. They sang hymns and other wonderful songs. While she admits that Kevin is the musically gifted one, Kim is thankful for their Christian upbringing and the freedom to express themselves through writing and singing. Kim was thrilled when the idea came to co-write with her brother, as it revived memories of a special time they had shared. Kim now spends her days as a creative writer. You may recognize some of her other books under the pen name of Sunnie Day. Kim retired from nursing after eighteen years, having worked in many areas of the medical field. She is the mother of four grown children and grandmother to five lovely grandchildren. Kim is married to Roy Thompson, and they reside in Texas.

Kevin Kruise served over twenty years in the United States Army and retired in February 2002. He is currently serving as a Department of the Army civilian in the United States Army Operational Test Command at Fort Hood, Texas. He holds a BS degree in History from Drury University and MA degree in Homeland Security from American Military University. Kevin has been married to Evelyn (Estepa) Kruise for over 22 years and has been blessed with four children and multiple grandchildren. Kevin is an active member at Grace Christian Center in Killeen, Texas, and serves on the worship ministry team as a guitarist. He has written many songs, poems, and short stories, but *God's Playbook* is his first published work.